W9-APN-891

No kiss had ever felt like this. So utterly right. So much more than a meeting of mouths.

Because this was *Niall*, the man Lola had fixated on more than half a lifetime ago and yearned for ever since.

"Niall." It was only as she heard the word that she registered the pressure of his mouth easing. His open lips brushed hers as he breathed deep, his chest pushing out against her.

Then his mouth was gone and she opened dazed eyes.

Cobalt eyes, impossibly bright, snared hers.

Her pulse thumped as something passed between them. A primal message that made her body tremble in anticipation.

es! At last!

ile trembled on her lips as sweet tenderness
h urgent arousal. Finally Niall recognized
force binding them together. The
o strong she hadn't been able to
it or batter it into submission
rying.

to, because Niall's eyes, and
ealed this was no longer a

Growing up near the beach, **Annie West** spent lots of time observing tall, burnished lifeguards—early research! Now she spends her days fantasizing about gorgeous men and their love lives. Annie has been a reader all her life. She also loves travel, long walks, good company and great food. You can contact her at annie@annie-west.com or via PO Box 1041, Warners Bay, NSW 2282, Australia.

Books by Annie West

Harlequin Presents

Contracted to Her Greek Enemy
Claiming His Out-of-Bounds Bride
The Sheikh's Marriage Proclamation
Pregnant with His Majesty's Heir
A Consequence Made in Greece

Sovereigns and Scandals

Revelations of a Secret Princess
The King's Bride by Arrangement

Visit the Author Profile page
at Harlequin.com for more titles.

Annie West

THE INNOCENT'S
PROTECTOR IN PARADISE

If you purchased this book without a cover you should be aware
that this book is stolen property. It was reported as "unsold and
destroyed" to the publisher, and neither the author nor the
publisher has received any payment for this "stripped book."

HARLEQUIN®
PRESENTS®

Recycling programs
for this product may
not exist in your area.

ISBN-13: 978-1-335-56920-2

The Innocent's Protector in Paradise

Copyright © 2021 by Annie West

All rights reserved. No part of this book may be used or reproduced in
any manner whatsoever without written permission except in the case of
brief quotations embodied in critical articles and reviews.

This is a work of fiction. Names, characters, places and incidents
are either the product of the author's imagination or are used fictitiously.
Any resemblance to actual persons, living or dead, businesses,
companies, events or locales is entirely coincidental.

This edition published by arrangement with Harlequin Books S.A.

For questions and comments about the quality of this book,
please contact us at CustomerService@Harlequin.com.

Harlequin Enterprises ULC
22 Adelaide St. West, 40th Floor
Toronto, Ontario M5H 4E3, Canada
www.Harlequin.com

Printed in U.S.A.

THE INNOCENT'S
PROTECTOR IN PARADISE

To three wonderful women who are always there when I need them:

Abby Green, Anna Campbell and Michelle Douglas.

Thank you!

PROLOGUE

'I'M WORRIED ABOUT LOLA. Something's seriously wrong but she won't tell me about it.'

Niall might have scoffed and asked how Ed could be sure there was a problem since his sister refused to share any details. But he trusted his best friend's judgement. Ed didn't worry over nothing.

Niall tucked the phone under his ear, turning to hear better over an airport announcement. 'What sort of wrong?'

'I don't know. She sounds…strained. You know what she's like. The world's worst liar. She tells me she's busy at work, but it's not that. The other day I heard a police siren in the background then she hung up quickly. When I asked later she said there'd been trouble in the street but her voice gave her away. Something's definitely wrong.'

Niall frowned. 'Police? You can't seriously think Lola's in strife with the cops.' Ed's little sister was the person least likely, ever, to commit a crime.

He remembered the first time he'd gone to the Suarez house with his new friend Ed after school.

Little Lola had solemnly surveyed him with big eyes as if, wisely, unsure whether to trust him. But then he did have a cut lip and the beginning of a black eye after that scuffle in the street. He'd felt as if Ed's kid sister had seen straight beneath his teenage bravado to the dark emptiness beneath.

It was only later that he discovered little Lola wasn't judging him. In fact, over time she came to treat him like another big brother. It was change she didn't like, and he, a troubled newcomer, was definitely that.

'Maybe if you were home in Melbourne instead of working away, she'd confide.' There were six years between Lola and Ed but they were close. As close as any siblings he'd known.

Niall pinched the bridge of his nose, ignoring a sudden slam of emotion.

'That's the problem,' Ed huffed. 'I *can't* get away. I'm in Antarctica for months yet. That's why I want you to check on her. You're heading to Melbourne, aren't you?'

'I'm at the airport now.' Niall stared through the plate glass window at the planes on the tarmac. 'I'll drop by to see her this evening, after my meetings.'

Niall didn't need to think twice about doing as Ed asked. He owed the Suarez family a debt he could never repay. Together they'd turned his life around when he teetered on the edge of self-destruction. If it hadn't been for them, his would have been a short journey from misfit teenager to gangs, violence and a quick end.

They'd reminded him that there were good things left in the world and encouraged him to dream big.

'I knew I could rely on you, mate. Thanks. Just… do whatever you need to look after her. She's her own worst enemy, thinks she always has to be strong and not lean on anyone.' Ed's sigh filled his ear.

'Don't worry. I'll keep the kid safe. I'm quite fond of her.'

Even if he hadn't seen her in years. Niall did a quick calculation. He'd last seen Lola when he went back to Melbourne for her mother's funeral. Lola had been just shy of her sixteenth birthday. Her sombre new clothes, bought, he guessed, for the funeral, and her bleak expression, had belonged to someone much older.

Niall had done what he could to comfort her, offering a hug and a shoulder to cry on, but she'd withdrawn into herself as if embarrassed to touch him. Her features, an intriguing amalgam of teenager and adult, had been stiff with rejection.

He'd understood. At a time like that it was family that counted. Not a stray who'd been informally adopted by her open-hearted parents. When you got down to it, he wasn't a Suarez. His past, his record with his own family, were appalling, even if he'd since made good professionally.

Niall rubbed his hand around the back of his neck, hearing his boarding call. He didn't fly south often. Melbourne held too many memories he preferred to forget. He spent most of his time in Brisbane or overseas.

He strolled to the gate. 'Leave it to me, Ed. I promise to look after her.' He paused. 'Lola's probably just got a new boyfriend she doesn't want you to know about yet.' Niall grinned, wondering what the kid looked like now. Her mother had been beautiful.

'Then I leave it to you to check him out, since that's your area of expertise. Just don't let her fob you off.'

Fob him off? Little Lola? The idea tugged Niall's mouth into a smile. The pretty airline attendant waiting for him blinked, then returned his smile with an eager grin.

CHAPTER ONE

YOU'RE JUMPING TO CONCLUSIONS. **Stay calm.**

But Lola's heart pounded so fast it felt as if it might take off. The heavy thrum vibrated through her chest like a helicopter rising from the ground.

She *was* certain.

Someone had been in her flat.

She felt it as soon as she entered. Switching on the light, she stopped in the doorway, trying to figure out what was wrong. Everything looked the same at first glance. Nothing disturbed.

Yet something registered as she took a deep calming breath. An unfamiliar chemical scent.

Lola stepped back out onto the landing, looking around, but couldn't see any sign of cleaning or maintenance work.

She hesitated in the doorway, contemplating calling the police again. That was what eventually drove her inside. Knowing they'd respond to her call but find nothing conclusive. The more she phoned in, the less urgent her calls would seem, like the boy who cried wolf.

That had happened to Therese.

Lola shivered, remembering her one-time neighbour.

So here she was, still in her work clothes, chilled to the bone despite the heating she'd turned on high, trying to decide how much danger she was in.

Had Braithwaite watched her enter the apartment block? She'd seen him, she was *sure* she'd seen him in the street these past weeks, though he'd disappeared quickly.

Had he watched her come into her flat tonight? Lola was sure she'd left the lounge room curtains closed when she went to work.

She crossed her arms, rubbing her hands up and down her sleeves, trying to get warm.

She went from room to room, checking the larger cupboards and under the bed, but she was alone.

Still she felt unnerved.

The doorbell rang and she jumped, nerves jangling.

It was half past seven and she wasn't expecting anyone. Her new neighbours kept to themselves. No dropping by for a chat or to borrow something.

Again it rang, the sound longer this time, as if whoever pressed the button knew she was in.

Braithwaite?

Lola froze, even stopped breathing for a moment as fear clamped its icy grip around her lungs and throat.

Had she locked the door?

Of course you did. You always do now.

Even so, her mind raced with awful imaginings of it opening and him coming in.

She grabbed her phone and thumbed in the emergency number just in case. Then she forced herself to walk the short hallway to the front door.

Gingerly, heart pounding an uneven tattoo, she peered through the spyhole.

It wasn't Braithwaite.

A relieved sigh eased from her lips.

She saw broad shoulders in a dark suit. A sliver of pale shirt collar and the back of a man's head. Glossy, black hair. Short hair, not like Braithwaite's. And Braithwaite wasn't as tall or broad-shouldered.

The man turned. His tie was askew as if he'd tugged it loose after a long day. He was too tall for her to see his eyes through the peephole, but she registered a firm, determined chin and a sensual mouth bracketed by grooves that should look grim yet instead made her insides flutter.

Lola's hand went to her throat. Her pulse hammered there as if her heart had risen from her ribcage, leaving her chest hollow.

No, not Braithwaite.

But another man she'd give almost anything not to see.

Niall Pedersen.

What was *he* doing here?

He made a habit of arriving when she was at her

most vulnerable. Last time had been for her mother's funeral.

Lola's mouth twisted with grim humour even as her belly curdled with pain and resentment. And a stubborn kernel of something else she still hadn't managed to eradicate and refused to think about.

She shut her eyes and counted to five, trying to shove down the wobbly, vulnerable feeling that everything was spinning out of control. She reached out and unlocked the door just as the buzzer sounded for a third time.

Niall filled the doorway. Had he been so broad across the shoulders eight years ago?

Lola told herself she couldn't remember, when in fact she had perfect recall.

Why did she stand, gawping up as if she'd never seen him before?

Because eight years had done more than fill out the lean promise of youth. It had given him an air of authority and assurance and etched new lines around his mouth and eyes that transformed a handsome youth into a man with serious charisma.

Lola's knees threatened to buckle and she hung onto the door handle, silently cursing.

He didn't know it but this man had blighted her life. She'd do well to remember it.

'Niall, this is unexpected.' Her voice was deeper than he'd expected and slightly husky. He felt it as a ripple of pleasure through his belly and a tingling awareness even lower.

For an instant he stared, mind blank while his hormones sped into overdrive. Until logic kicked in.

Lola. Ed's kid sister. The girl he'd come to help. Girl no longer. She was a woman now.

Niall swallowed, amazed to feel his throat constrict.

He'd known she'd be different. He just hadn't reckoned on how different.

'Lola.' He managed, just, to keep the question from his voice. As if, even knowing it had to be her, he couldn't reconcile the sweet, serious kid he'd known with this woman. 'It's good to see you.'

His gaze skated over her dark grey pencil skirt to long legs in shimmery hose and high heels. His smile solidified as he followed svelte curves then returned to her face.

She'd grown into her nose and her wide mouth. And those eyes, that had once made her look like a serious little owl, were the lustrous eyes of a beautiful woman.

She looked stern and sexy at the same time. As if her rigidly pulled-back hair and business suit camouflaged a sultry woman who…

Niall stiffened, horrified. This was *Lola*! He did *not* think about Ed's little sister that way.

Even so, he wished his mate had warned him. All these years when he'd mentioned Lola he'd never once hinted she'd turned into a stunner.

Of course she's altered. It's been almost a decade.
Yet Niall felt sideswiped by the change in her.

'What are you—?' she began.

'Are you going to invite me—?' he said at the same time.

Her lips flattened, surprising him. For she, and the rest of the Suarez family, had always been generously hospitable. Then her expression changed, her mouth tilted up at the corners as she stepped back and waved him in. 'Please, come in.'

It was only as he passed her that he saw the phone in her hand, her thumb hovering over the call button.

'Have I come at a bad time?'

A second's hesitation then she shook her head. Yet she didn't meet his eyes as she shut and locked the door behind him.

'No, I've just got home and wasn't expecting anyone.'

'You work long hours,' he observed, trying not to focus on the movement of her hips beneath the tailored skirt as he followed her into a sitting room.

Niall looked around curiously. The place was furnished in soothing pale greens and white. Except for one bright pop of colour, a tumble of cushions on the sofa in bright orange and bronze. A bookcase was stacked full, the bottom shelves with big, serious-looking books on management and finance and the top with fiction titles.

'I've got a big project on at the moment. I'm sure

you know how it is. You didn't get where you are by working nine to five.'

Niall nodded. 'True.' He'd worked hard for his success, CEO of a multibillion-dollar enterprise in his early thirties.

He waited for her to take a seat, but she stood in the entrance to the room, shoulders high and hands clasped as if not sure what to do with them.

Strange. The way she dressed, and the confident sway of her body as she'd strode down the hallway, projected an assured, capable woman. But the vibe he got was something else. His eyes narrowed. Was she biting the corner of her mouth?

It was something she used to do when nervous.

Time telescoped and for a second he was back in the Suarez family kitchen, watching little Lola fret over a school assignment. She'd been convinced she'd fail, till Niall took pity on her and checked it for her, reassuring her she'd not only pass but do brilliantly.

'I'm in Melbourne on business and wondered if you'd like to go to dinner. I don't get here often and thought it would be good to catch up.'

'Dinner?' She looked at him as if she'd never heard the word before. Not the reaction he usually got when he asked a woman out.

'I realise it's short notice.'

'I… That's very kind of you.' She flashed a smile that didn't reach her eyes. 'Any other time and I'd love to. But it's been a long day and I have an early start tomorrow.'

'I understand.' Yet his sixth sense, alerted by Ed's call, told him there was something more than tiredness here. Which was why he didn't take the hint and leave. After all, they were as good as family. 'How about we order some food in? I can organise it while you get out of your office clothes.' His gaze strayed of its own volition to her slender legs in those heels and he yanked it back up again.

'Oh!' He could see her trying to think of a reason to refuse.

'Just a quick meal.' He reassured her. 'I've got a heavy schedule tomorrow myself.' He sweetened the words with a smile and watched her blink. The tightness around her mouth eased a little.

Warmth filled him. This wasn't just about a favour to Ed. He mightn't have seen Lola in years but he still cared about her. He saw faint shadows beneath her eyes and concern stirred.

'Thank you. But—'

'Unless you're expecting someone. A boyfriend maybe?'

'No. No boyfriend.' Her eyes widened a little as if surprised she'd let the words slip.

Niall felt a punch of something that might have been satisfaction. Because he could at least report to Ed that there was no guy turning Lola's life upside down.

'I'd like to hear what you're doing these days.' He

paused. 'And I'd love company. Being in the city has brought back a lot of memories.' It was true. His spine had been stiff all day as the ghosts of the past followed him.

He spread his hands and offered a rueful smile. She didn't know his whole story, but enough to understand there were dark shadows over his early years. Not even Ed knew all the details.

Niall saw her waver, her desire to be alone fighting her soft heart.

She nodded abruptly. 'That would be...nice. I could do with company too.' Then she smiled. A genuine smile that clogged his airways for a second.

Because Niall was still getting used to this new Lola. Once the novelty wore off, he'd go back to thinking of her as he always had. Little Lola.

Not as a disturbingly attractive woman.

'Excellent. What sort of food do you want?'

'There's a great Thai place down the road. The menu's on the fridge. Help yourself.' She spun on her heel and headed towards her bedroom.

The lights were already on in the gleaming kitchen. He stood in the doorway, noting that in this at least she hadn't changed. Lola wasn't obsessive, but the difference between her space and Ed's had always been a family joke. Ed thrived on clutter while Lola had everything in its right place.

It was good to know she hadn't changed completely. She'd always been organised and thoughtful. Tender-hearted too, hence her being swayed by his apparent need for company. And determined. When she set her mind to something she didn't give up.

Here there was no clutter. The pristine white was softened by a row of potted herbs along the windowsill. Niall passed them then paused.

Something smelled odd.

He retraced his steps then leaned across, inhaling. Slowly he turned first one pot around then another and another.

Each plant was dead on the side that had faced the window. Not gradually ageing, but green and alive on one side and completely dead and shrivelled on the other. The difference between the two halves was a clear line straight down the middle.

He leaned forward and an acrid odour hit his nostrils. He jerked back, grimacing.

Something noxious had been put on each plant. But so neatly it might have been done using a ruler.

Niall frowned. Lola wouldn't make a mistake like that. She'd always had a green thumb, helping her mother in the garden.

His nape prickled as he stared at the damaged plants. Poisoned, if he guessed correctly. That was what he smelled. The lingering scent of acid.

He could think of no sane reason why Lola would half poison her plants. Especially ones she used in cooking.

His sixth sense stirred. The one that had kept him alive in his teens when he'd hung with a crowd that was rougher and more dangerous than he. That instinct had saved him more than once. Nowadays the closest he came to experiencing it was as a frisson of excitement that told him a new software break-through, or a new business opportunity, promised success.

He stood still, surveying the kitchen.

Everything gleamed and even the single flyer on the fridge sat precisely square. A blue and white checked tea towel hung neatly over the oven's han-dle. The benchtop was clear except for a blue bowl full of winter oranges, a gleaming stainless-steel electric jug and an empty, clear glass teapot.

No, not empty. As Niall turned he caught sight of something that glinted.

He stepped back and saw he was mistaken. The teapot was empty, ready for the next brew. Yet that warning niggle persisted. He swept his gaze around the kitchen, then reached for the teapot and pulled the lid off.

Niall carried it directly under the kitchen light, surveying the clear residue in the bottom of the vessel.

Every hair on his neck and arms stood up as he inspected the tiny grains. He touched them with his index finger and lifted it for closer inspection.

Not sugar, as he'd first thought.

Ground glass.

Someone had sabotaged Lola's kitchen horrifi-cally. If she'd made tea, not really paying attention, she'd have taken the lid off the pot, added tea then water, and poured herself a cup laced with glass.

Niall shuddered. Whoever had done this hadn't just planned to scare Lola. Her tormentor meant to do serious harm. It didn't matter that, contrary to common belief, this wasn't likely to be lethal. What mattered was the guy's intent. That was more than ugly. *It was murderous.*

Niall slammed the teapot onto the bench and seconds later was pounding on her closed bedroom door.

'Lola? Are you okay?'

Silence. His imagination ran riot. If someone had sabotaged her kitchen, what about her bedroom?

Grabbing the handle, he turned it and shoved, just as she pulled it open. Niall's momentum took him across the threshold, straight into Lola.

His heart slammed his ribs, relief filling him as his hands closed around her. Soft curves pressed into him as he absorbed her scented warmth.

She was safe.

'Niall? What's going on?' She scowled up at him, eyes narrowing as she reared back.

Reluctantly he released her, fighting another instinct. This one urged him to pull her hard against him and keep her there.

Protectiveness?

Or a compulsion that sprang not from anything so pure, but from his primal response to her soft femininity in that split second of full body contact?

The insight stunned him.

Niall gritted his jaw and stepped back, putting more distance between them.

She's fine, he assured himself.

Actually she was more than fine, in slim-fitting jeans and a soft green sweater that drew his eyes to her willowy frame.

'Sorry. I didn't mean to barge in. Is everything okay here?'

He forced himself to look past her, taking in the feminine room. The antique mirror and the collection of delicate fans in custom-made glass-fronted frames on one wall. The floor-to-ceiling wardrobe. The cream-covered bed, strewn with ruby-red cushions.

'Why wouldn't it be?' Yet her voice betrayed her. Lola was nervous.

Niall's gaze fixed on her lovely features. She was too pale and once more she gnawed on her lip. 'Are you going to tell me what's going on?'

Lola's chin shot up but she couldn't look him in the eye. 'I don't know what you mean.'

Tell him!

And what's he going to do? He lives at the other end of the country. He can't protect you. He'll just fuss and tell Ed who'll then fret because he's not here.

'Someone's been in your apartment.'

Her eyes widened. Reluctantly she looked up

from that sexy mouth and uncompromising chin to navy-blue eyes that even after eight years still had the power to undo her.

Something deep, deep within crumpled.

The hope she'd clung to, that by now she'd have shed this unwanted crush, faded, leaving her floundering.

Lola breathed deep, marshalling her thoughts. How could she even think about her response to Niall at a time like this?

Because fixating on all that raw masculinity was preferable to thinking about the danger she was in. The danger the police seemed unable to tackle.

She was terrified. She'd been scared for weeks and it was wearing her out.

Lola took another breath and clawed back some control.

'How do you know?' She'd been here a full five minutes before Niall and hadn't been able to pin-point what was different about the place. Apart from the smell.

'I'll show you in a moment.' His brows gathered in a frown. 'You know who it was, don't you?' Niall's expression morphed from concerned to angry. 'Is it a man? Did you give him a key?'

No, not angry. *Furious.*

As if it were her fault that she was being stalked! The realisation snapped her out of shocked stasis.

'No. I didn't give anyone a key.'

Black eyebrows rose and his mobile mouth pulled

into a grimace that spoke of distaste. 'Okay. How about someone you invited back here. Someone who stayed the night. They could have taken an impression of your key when you weren't looking and got a spare made.'

That was a laugh.

There'd been no men in her life, not in that sense.

Not for want of trying on Lola's part. The thought mocked her. But no matter how hopeful she was when agreeing to a date, it inevitably failed to lead anywhere. For no man lived up to the ideal she'd built in her head.

Her fault, she knew. And this man's.

That, alone, was reason to hate him.

'You really don't have much faith in my judgement, do you?' If anything, she set her standards too high. It was a problem she'd tried, and failed, to rectify.

Her gaze skated across those straight shoulders, taking in his lean body that looked so athletic and potently masculine.

Lola shut her eyes, willing herself to concentrate.

'Just tell me. How do you know someone's been here?' She opened her eyes to find him canting towards her, his eyes fixed on her mouth. Heat drilled down, filling her with melting sensations she wished she could feel with some other man. *Any* other man!

Niall straightened, his expression grim. 'Come.' He stood back and led the way to the kitchen.

Relieved, she followed, eager to shift her focus. The room looked the same as ever, except…

Lola gasped when she saw her herbs. That faint smell was stronger here, strong enough that as she got close it caught the back of her throat.

Or maybe that was fear.

Her eyes widened as she saw the withered foliage. No, not withered. Burnt. He'd burnt them with acid.

Lola's hand went to her mouth as she gagged, remembering what had happened to Therese. The sear of acid on flesh. Lola's other arm wrapped around her middle as her insides cramped, stomach curdling. A cry of horror escaped before she could stop it.

It was Braithwaite. Not her imagination, as the last police officer had tried to convince her.

'Lola? Lola!' Strong arms encircled her and pulled her close. Niall was tall and taut with muscle. For a few seconds she stood stiff and unresisting, afraid that leaning on him felt too easy when she had to remain strong.

But as Niall's heat seeped into her, inevitably she sagged against him, the great shudders racking her gradually subsiding into tremors.

It felt like a lifetime since she'd let herself relax. She'd been on alert so long. How long since she'd stood this close to someone? Not since her dad took off on his round-Australia camping trip six months ago.

'It's okay, Lola.' Niall's deep voice resonated through her as she leaned against him.

She opened her mouth to say it wasn't okay. It was a horrible, frightening mess. Instead she shut her eyes and let her head rest against him. Nestled here, it wasn't acid she smelled but cedar, spice and warm male. Lola drank it in greedily.

One large hand slowly circled her back. A gesture of comfort that eased the knot of unbearable tension she'd carried high in her chest for weeks.

Finally, when the temptation never to move grew too strong, she lifted her head. Somehow her arms had gone around Niall, circling tight as if clutching at safety. Hastily she released him, stepping back.

At least now her heart wasn't hammering in her throat. The panic had edged down to manageable levels.

'Sorry, Niall. I'm not usually so...' She shrugged, preferring not to put into words her vulnerability.

'Don't apologise.' His voice was gruff and she watched his chest rise on a deep breath. Finally she lifted her gaze to his face and her newfound sense of strength ebbed.

'What is it? Is there something else?' His expression was so grim, fear feathered her spine.

'Isn't that enough? Come on, let's get you out of here.'

'Out?' Lola frowned. 'I need to call the police. Report an intruder.'

Niall was already ushering her out of the kitchen.

'Of course. But it doesn't have to be now. Tomorrow during business hours will do. I'll make sure the place is secure so no one can enter in the meantime.'

It was tempting, the thought of walking away and leaving this for tomorrow. It had been a long, trying day, and the police interview would make it longer. She already felt exhausted.

'My car's outside. We can get you a bed where I'm staying and forget all this till the morning.'

Impossible to forget, but how she longed to escape this nightmare, even if for one night. Maybe then she'd find her usual energy and determination.

She looked into that concerned dark blue stare and was suddenly glad Niall had come. 'I'll pack a bag.'

CHAPTER TWO

NIALL WATCHED HER go to her room and released a slow breath. A shudder of frustration and fury coursed through him. Fury at what had happened and frustration that he didn't have a quick fix for Lola.

Why had Ed waited so long to help her? Her brother, or someone, should have been looking out for her!

Whoever had done this had, judging by Lola's response, been active before. He guessed she knew the intruder.

His belly clenched. Was it an ex-lover? Someone Lola had been intimate with? Nausea stirred.

He grimaced. He had trouble imagining her with a man. Not because she wasn't attractive but...

Because he wanted that man to be him?

Her slender body, sultry mouth and combination of feistiness and softness made him ache in places he shouldn't. That was wrong in so many ways. Self-disgust filled him and he told himself it was the shock of seeing her all grown up. It couldn't be anything more. He wouldn't allow it.

Yet it was beyond him to think of this as simply a protection job. The sort his staff dealt with regularly. He'd wanted to scoop Lola into his arms and tell her it would be all right. That he'd look after her.

A pang of old, familiar guilt knifed his gut. The fear that, once more, he would fail in his duty. But he ignored it. He couldn't dwell on past mistakes now.

That desire to protect had stopped him telling Lola about the ground glass. About the immediate physical threat. The intruder hadn't just wanted to scare her. He'd intended serious physical harm.

Niall had been on the point of telling her then decided against it. Even as a child, Lola had done a good job of appearing calm when she was worried. She hated admitting she was out of her depth. Yet those acid-damaged plants had undone her totally. Clearly she'd been at the end of her tether.

The sight of her dazed hazel eyes, more brown than green, and dull with distress, had twisted his vitals. The feel of her, shaking as she burrowed against him, the way she'd clung…

How could he add to her fear by revealing the cruel trap set for her?

Time enough later, when she was calm and rested.

Glancing at the bedroom door, Niall moved away and pulled out his phone. Pedersen Security's Melbourne office was staffed twenty-four hours a day, seven days a week. Securing the premises till the police arrived tomorrow was easily done.

As he issued his instructions, low-voiced, he began searching. For that sixth sense still hummed. It told him there was more to find.

What else had the bastard left? Another boobytrap?

A couple of minutes later he found it. Not a boobytrap but a camera concealed high in the hallway.

It wasn't the highest spec. Not the sort of equipment his own company supplied. But it would do the job, giving an unseen watcher a clear view of the lounge room and the bedroom and bathroom doorways.

Ice crackled along his bones. Yet it did nothing to quench the searing wrath in his belly.

How long had the camera been there?

Were there more? In the bathroom perhaps?

Pain cracked through Niall's jaw and he realised he was grinding his teeth.

He wanted to get his hands on whoever was doing this.

A noise made him turn and there was Lola, emerging from the bedroom with an overnight bag and a laptop. She looked slender and defenceless, despite her pushed-back shoulders and calm expression.

Too calm. Her eyes betrayed her as did the tremor in her hand as she hitched her shoulder bag up.

Niall strode forward and took the overnight case.

'All ready?' He forced a reassuring note to his voice and saw the tight pinch of her mouth ease.

'Yes, let's get out of here.'

He nodded and opened the door for her. He'd promised Ed that he'd keep her safe. He'd keep that promise, no matter what it took.

Niall knew the consequences of failure too well. He refused to live with another life on his conscience.

He'd protect Lola and stop whoever was hurting her.

She wouldn't come back until he knew it was completely safe.

Lola had spent the drive into the city in a fog of anxiety and anger. It was only when Niall pulled up at the entrance to Melbourne's grandest hotel that she blinked and realised where she was.

By then a uniformed staff member was opening the car for her while another stood before huge gilt and glass doors, where a crimson carpet led into a stunning atrium.

Niall's a billionaire. Of course he stays at the best.

Yet it took Lola by surprise. When she thought of him it wasn't his wealth that came to mind, or the astronomical success he'd achieved following his breakthrough, developing security software that had revolutionised the industry.

Lola knew all about it because she'd followed his success via Ed's updates and the press reports. He was a favourite subject, since his small Brisbane security firm had grown into an international success story. And because he was perfect fodder for the media, handsome, rich and with an endless supply of gorgeous blonde companions.

She tried to gather her thoughts, watching Niall speak to a porter, refusing assistance with her bag.

He was unfazed by the grand surroundings. She, on the other hand, felt rumpled and out of place. She longed for somewhere quiet and cosy to regroup, not this palatial place.

Niall had never been cowed by anything. Neither authority figures nor brute force. As a teenager he'd stood up to school bullies. For a while it seemed he was always in fights. On the other hand he'd taken time to help her with her homework and let her hang around while he and Ed tinkered on old computers or while he practised martial arts.

He'd been like another brother.

But it was a long time since she'd thought of him like that.

'Ready?' There it was. A warmth in those dark blue eyes that she recognised from years ago. When she'd hung on his every word and he'd responded with infinite patience.

Maybe he'd never noticed her massive crush. She could only hope.

'Yes.' Lola hefted her laptop case and hitched her shoulder bag, preceding him.

Instead of going to the reception desk, Niall led her towards a bank of lifts.

'I need to check in.'

The doors slid open with a discreet ping and he ushered her inside.

'There's plenty of room in my suite. You can have a shower or bath while I order dinner. That way you don't have to go anywhere or do anything until tomorrow.'

It was a sign of how shattered she felt that it sounded like paradise. Lola's protest died.

That was how, thirty minutes later, she found herself in the most luxurious bathroom she'd ever seen, staring out of the full-length window at the city lights. Niall's suite was an apartment-style penthouse with a view of the Yarra River winding through the CBD.

Her little flat and all her troubles seemed a world away.

Except for the burr of apprehension beneath her skin. Even the long, hot shower, the ruthless scrubbing of hair and skin, couldn't eradicate the taint of fear.

She tasted it still on her tongue.

With a moue of self-disgust she cinched the belt of the soft-as-a-cloud plush robe she'd found. It was crazy but she couldn't bring herself to put her jeans and sweater on again, though she'd only worn them half an hour.

Because they made her think of that ravaged

scene in her kitchen. Lola shut her eyes, catching again the pungent scent of acid.

She snapped her eyes open and saw herself in the mirror. Face too pale. Scared, mud-coloured eyes. Her hair several shades darker from being wet and already beginning to curl. But she didn't have the energy to straighten it.

After all, she wasn't dressing to impress Niall.

No matter what feminine pride urged.

Sweeping up her clothes, she entered the bed-room. The door on the far side was open and through it she saw Niall, pacing the massive lounge room as he spoke, low-voiced, on the phone.

Lola didn't think she'd made any noise but in-stantly his head turned, dark eyes snaring hers.

It was nonsense to believe that stare stopped her in her tracks. Or sent awareness sizzling through her. Or snagged the breath in her lungs, making them tight.

She was over him. Had been over him for years.

Her mouth lifted in a rueful grimace. There was nothing to get over. There'd never been anything between them. Just juvenile hopes that should have died a natural death by now.

Besides, Niall had always been drawn to curvy blondes, never mediocre brunettes. In his teens that bias had been a bit of a joke between him and Ed. But his preference had lasted, proven by every press photo of him with a gorgeous woman at his side, and Ed's comments about his friend's predictability.

Niall only dated blondes. Glamorous, sophisticated blondes. He would never look at her and think *desirable woman*. Even if she dyed her hair, which she wasn't planning, she'd never manage the sophisticated, overtly glamorous style he favoured. Or the bombshell body.

She was happy as she was. She wasn't pining for Niall any more.

Lola turned away, rummaging in her bag for something to wear. She didn't have much choice. It was tomorrow's work clothes or pyjamas.

She reached for the long pyjamas, plain white flannelette with a sprinkling of red hearts. Plain white buttons down the loose-fitting shirt. Her grim smile turned into a husky laugh that made her throat ache. This was as far from slinky, enticing lingerie as you could get.

'Dinner's ready if you are.' Niall stood in the doorway, his expression unreadable.

Even so, Lola felt suddenly hyper-conscious of the way the plush robe rubbed against her nipples, thighs and stomach as she moved. A snaking tendril of awareness writhed in that hollow place between her thighs.

People said sexual arousal was common after danger. It was a survival instinct. And, though Braithwaite hadn't put her in physical danger, it felt that way.

That was the simplest, the only acceptable explanation of her response to feeling Niall's gaze, heavy as a touch on her body.

'I'll be ready in a moment.'

Lola refused to share a meal with him wearing nothing but a robe, even if it covered her from neck to knee.

'Very cute,' he murmured minutes later when she pulled a chair up to the table where he'd put an array of covered plates.

'Sorry?'

'The hearts.' He nodded to the collar of her thick pyjamas, visible behind the V-neck of her robe. 'They're cute.'

Lola opened her mouth to tell him women didn't want to be called cute, then realised that might invite speculation on what she did want to hear. She busied herself lifting the lids keeping the food warm.

'I hope you're hungry. There's enough here to feed an army.'

He shrugged and she fought not to stare. With his tailored jacket off and sleeves rolled up Niall looked too accessible and attractive for her peace of mind.

'I wasn't sure what you liked so I chose a variety. As I recall you have a healthy appetite.'

Which was a polite way of saying she'd comfort eaten through puberty.

Niall probably thought of her as she'd been at twelve or thirteen. Chubby and frumpy with her home-made clothes that she was always either growing into or out of. The flannel pyjamas would reinforce the image.

For a second she wished she'd packed a whisper-thin nightie and matching robe of black lace, sexy and alluring. Except she didn't look good in black and she didn't have anything like that in her wardrobe.

How nice it would be, just once, to steal Niall's breath. To have him think her impossibly irresistible.

Dream on, Lola!

Determined, she forced herself to concentrate on the food, taking a sample of everything and telling herself she needed to refuel. The last few days had been frantic at work and at home she'd been too unsettled to cook a proper meal. Maybe that was why tonight's events made her feel so weak and worried.

Or it could be because Braithwaite actually got into your flat!

If he'd been inside when you got home...

She shivered and put her cutlery down with a clatter, horror glazing her vision and tightening her throat.

'Are you ready to tell me about it?'

The words were smooth, as if Niall had an unquestionable right to know everything.

Lola was used to being the capable one. The one who looked after others, not the one needing care.

For a second she felt again that horrible sense of total helplessness, when the world had turned on its head. It had engulfed her when she was a teenager. Her mother had died and her father, lost without his other half, had numbed the pain with a catastrophic drinking and gambling binge, losing his job, almost losing the house, and heading towards self-destruction. Ed had been away at university and didn't see everything. It had been left to Lola to support her dad and help him find a way out, back to the real world.

She'd find a way out of this. She had to.
She refused to let Braithwaite destroy her.

'Lola?' A warm, callused hand covered hers. 'You don't have to tell me now. But you need to know I'll do whatever it takes to keep you safe. I promise.'

She raised her eyes and blinked to clear her vision.

Niall looked as serious as she'd ever seen him. As if the sight of her so troubled got under his skin. He'd always been protective.

But she'd learnt to rely on herself. To solve her own problems, in the process becoming a stalwart for others when things went wrong.

Yet she was weary. So tired of being strong.

Niall deserved some explanation, even if his protection could only be short term while he visited Melbourne. They said talking was therapeutic. Lola had lost track of the number of friends who, over the years, had come to her for a shoulder to cry on.

Nevertheless she hesitated. Sharing this would

invite Niall into her private life. A place she'd tried and failed to keep free of his shadow.

'Thanks, Niall. It's kind of you to go to so much effort for someone you don't even know any more.'

His eyebrows soared. 'I know it's been a while, Lola, but surely we're still friends.'

Was that a shadow of hurt in his eyes? Surely not. Niall was a tough, self-made tycoon with the world at his feet. He wouldn't fret over old ties.

Except, according to Ed, Niall was closer to the Suarez family than he was to his estranged father, his only living relative. Perhaps Lola wasn't the only one for whom those golden years when her parents had welcomed Niall into their family were special.

'Of course.'

'And you trust me.' His gaze held hers and it felt as if something powerful passed between them. Something more than shared memories. 'Like a brother.'

How Lola wished that were true. She did trust him. But as a brother? Not given the effect he had on her hormones.

Still.

Always.

Despair scoured her and she looked away, desperate for something else to focus on.

Too much had happened today. Her emotions were too close to the surface.

He lifted a bottle of wine towards her glass in silent question. Her eyes rounded as she read the label. It was an iconic Australian Shiraz she'd never had the money to order and probably never would. Another reminder that Niall Pedersen now lived in a completely different world.

She nodded. A lovely smooth glass of red would warm her against the chill still frosting her bones. 'Yes, please.'

Lola ate a forkful of steaming beef and mushroom pie, her eyes closing in appreciation of the rich flavour and the buttery, flaky texture of fresh-made pastry.

The food was delicious and, to her surprise, so was the companionable atmosphere that gradually developed. Niall gave up prodding and settled in to share the meal with her, chatting across a range of subjects that didn't require much input. Slowly she felt herself sink further into her comfortable chair.

It was as Niall poured her a second glass of the gorgeous wine that she made up her mind to tell him. Possibly because he hadn't kept pushing but respected her need for peace.

Besides, she discovered, she *wanted* to share with him. Maybe because he'd be gone soon. It would be like unburdening herself to a stranger she wouldn't see again.

She took a slow sip of the Shiraz, enjoying its mellow flavour and her burgeoning sense of comfort. How different from the stress of the last weeks.

'His name is Braithwaite. Jayden Braithwaite. He's…' she paused, remembering her last police interview and the insistence on facts '… I *think* he's stalking me.'

'How do you know him?' Instead of watching her, Niall concentrated on buttering a crusty bread roll. Because he knew it was easier to talk about difficult things without being stared at?

'He used to live next door. He was my ex-neighbour, Therese's partner.'

Dark eyes snared hers. 'Your neighbour's partner?'

Did Lola imagine the stress on the word *neighbour*? She frowned.

'Braithwaite wasn't my type.' She shuddered and took another small sip from her glass.

Niall said nothing, just nodded and turned his attention to the bread.

'Over time Therese became scared. He grew controlling, even over simple things like talking to neighbours or going to buy groceries. Things escalated and he became violent.' Lola paused, remembering the sound of screams and falling furniture. 'She kicked him out.'

'But he didn't stay away?'

Lola slanted a look into that dark, intent face.

'He stalked her. Made her life hell. She never knew when he was going to appear. He sent letters begging her to let him move back and at the same time posted flyers in the neighbourhood and to her colleagues at work, saying awful things about her.'

'And the police?'

'Said they didn't have enough evidence. They couldn't get DNA evidence linking him to the letters and posters. Even when the attacks got worse, slashed car tyres, disgusting things sent through the mail...' Lola rubbed her hands up and down her arms. 'Finally, he caught her walking to her car and threw acid over her.'

Niall swore, low and savage, and for some reason the sound eased Lola's distress.

'How is she?'

Lola shrugged. 'She survived. She turned when she saw him and the acid only hit her arm and shoulder. That was bad enough. It's not just physical scars she carries.' Lola's voice choked off.

'You were there?' Once more that firm hand covered hers and she was glad of the contact.

'I was on my balcony and saw what happened. I managed to snap a photo of him. It was one of the reasons they finally managed to lock him away.'

'So he blames you for his prison sentence?'

She nodded jerkily. 'He somehow got a lenient sentence and he's recently been released. Therese moved away and changed her name but I'm in the same place. I've seen him a couple of times. I know it's him. I just can't prove he's following me.'

'Tonight's not the first time he's bothered you?'

Lola sank back in her chair, but that lovely mellow feeling was gone. 'It's been weeks.' Fraught weeks as she wound tighter and tighter trying to anticipate what he'd do next.

Niall turned her hand over on the table and threaded his fingers through hers. His were longer and stronger, yet their joined hands felt matched. Lola looked down at them, wondering why that should be.

But then her nerves were stretched thin. Any re-assuring touch would feel good.

'He's been following you. What else?'

She shivered and he squeezed her hand. Strange how that simple reassurance made it easier to gather her shredded self-control.

'I've got a list on the computer with dates, times and photos.'

'He sent you mail?'

'No. But there are other things.'

She hurried on, giving a truncated version. 'It started with phone calls at all hours of the night. Then the feeling I was being followed. Nuisance phone calls at work. Messages that my father or Ed had been in an accident, dragging me out of meetings to deal with emergencies that didn't exist.' She'd been overwhelmed with relief each time, but her stress levels had steadily built and never had a chance to reduce.

'Damage to my front door. Then a cricket ball through the bedroom window.'

'Were you hurt?' His fingers tightened around hers.

'I wasn't home.'

'What did the police say?'

She shrugged. 'I'm only one floor up. They said it could have been kids playing.'

'And the damage to the door?'

'Vandals. There was nothing to link it to Braithwaite.'

'What else?'

'A dead mouse in the letter box. Then a dead rat on the balcony.' Lola reached for her glass, swirling the dark liquid. 'My cat, well, Therese's cat, but I adopted it when she moved...it got run over. I found it on the footpath when I got home last night.'

Needing time, she sipped her wine, but now it tasted sour. She put it down and pulled her hand free of Niall's.

It was time to regroup. Be strong. Niall wouldn't be around to fight her battles. That was up to her.

'The incidents have been escalating.'

Her head jerked up, her gaze colliding with his. That was what had scared her—what came next.

'Yes. Then today...' She didn't finish. The thought of that man in her home made her sick. 'You said you'd secure the flat tonight. I should have asked—'

'Don't fret about it. Pedersen Security staff are guarding it till the police come tomorrow. After that, we'll install better locks and ongoing security.'

Niall made it seem easy.

She had no idea about security systems. All she knew was that she never again wanted to discover Braithwaite had been in her space.

'Thank you. You're very kind.'

Something flashed across his sculpted features. 'It's nothing. Easily taken care of.'

His tone told her Niall understood how serious this was. He was anything but dismissive.

Lola exhaled slowly, relieved that at last there was someone who understood. The police had varied from disbelieving to sympathetic but pessimistic about proving Braithwaite's involvement.

She hadn't given her work colleagues the full story, not wanting to be seen as a helpless victim starring in some ongoing drama. She'd worked incredibly hard to build her strong professional reputation. She didn't want to distract people from that when she stood on the cusp of what might be her big break. Her bosses would be sympathetic, but she wanted them to think of her as a rising star, not someone needing sympathy.

'Thanks for listening,' she murmured. 'It's good to get it off my chest.' It felt as if someone had loosened a tight band around her ribs. Her breath came more easily.

'What are friends for?' He lifted his glass and took a long sip. 'It turns out my meetings tomorrow are starting late. While you're talking to the police, I'll make the necessary arrangements. We'll keep you safe until your stalker is dealt with. You have my word on it.'

CHAPTER THREE

LOLA HUFFED OUT a tired breath. The office was empty this late on a Friday and she'd worked on overdrive to wrap up everything.

After starting the day with the police, she'd been way behind when she got to work and barely had enough time to run through her part of the presentation before it began.

At least work was an antidote to her anxiety over Braithwaite. The semi-permanent frisson of anxiety rippling under her skin had eased with today's good news.

A smile tugged her mouth. She still couldn't believe it. The proposal hadn't just been approved, they'd been complimented on their innovative approach.

Her first creative project!

She might work for an advertising agency but her expertise was in administration. She'd left school early and begun as an office junior, climbing to become office administrator despite being only in her mid-twenties.

She was practical, meticulous and good with people—it had seemed like her destiny. Except over the years she'd been fascinated by the work going on around her, absorbing information, even studying on the side.

Until an account manager, short-staffed and desperate, had let her help out. That had fed her interest and she'd discovered to her surprise that she wasn't just the methodical organiser she'd always thought. She had creative instincts itching to be tested.

Lola had no illusions. She had a long way to go if she really wanted to shift her career direction, but getting approval to assist in a small way on this new campaign was a start. A chance to gauge if it really was what she wanted to do, and if she had the potential to succeed.

She'd have to work doubly hard and maybe she didn't have what it took. But after all these years, she longed for the chance to try.

Her phone rang. 'Lola?'

Niall Pedersen. His rich voice turned her good intentions inside out. Intentions to sever ties to the man who still affected her as he had when she was a teenager.

Last night she'd been sucked into the warmth of his caring, allowing herself to forget how dangerous he was to her equilibrium.

She stifled a bitter laugh. Two men in her life, both unwanted, both dangerous but in totally different ways.

'Hi, Niall. Finished your meetings?'

He'd suggested they meet after work and she'd been unable to refuse. Not after all his help.

He'd been there when the police came to the flat this morning, staying on with the key when she had to get to the office. He'd generously organised state-of-the-art security for her flat, staring down her insistence that he send her the bill, saying it would be an insult to accept payment.

'I'm waiting out the front. Whenever you're ready.'

'I'll be down in five.'

Swiftly saving the changes to her document, Lola shut down her computer and slipped on the shoes she'd kicked off. She refreshed her lip gloss and checked her hair was still in its chignon, then realised what she was doing. And that her pulse was racing.

She'd always been careful of her appearance at work, dressing for success with scrupulously straightened and styled hair. She allowed no unruly curls and dressed smartly but in muted colours. What had begun in her teens as an attempt to look older and more experienced had become habit.

There's no one to see you but Niall.

Are you primping for him?

He's not collecting you for a date. He'll never look at you that way. You're just Ed's little sister. An obligation.

Lola paused in the act of smoothing her skirt down her thighs. Her hands trembled.

She tried to tell herself it was weariness and reaction to the stress she'd been under.

But she couldn't swallow the lie. Logic told her it would be better when Niall flew back to his home thousands of kilometres to the north. Then she could focus, again, on trying to forget him. On dealing with this work opportunity and Braithwaite. Yet a needy part of her whispered that she didn't want him to leave.

It made no difference what she wanted. It never had. She'd see him, thank him, get her key and go home. Though the thought of returning to her flat held little appeal. If Braithwaite continued to target her she'd have to move. But would that stop him or would he find her again?

Rain lashed the street, a solid wall of dismal winter. But parked directly before the entrance was a familiar black sedan.

This time when Niall left she'd find a way to put him behind her. This time she'd succeed.

'Lola.' She swung around, her hand going to her throat.

Beside the entry, Niall stepped close, holding a furled umbrella. Tiny drops of moisture clung like crystals to his black hair. In jeans and a dark sweater he looked big and reassuring and far too attractive.

'I didn't see you.'

He frowned. 'You came outside without looking? What if Braithwaite had been here instead of me?'

Lola swallowed her instinctive protest. He was right.

'Usually I'm much more careful.' She bit her lip. For weeks she'd watched every step. Only tonight, thinking of Niall, she'd been distracted. Proof, if she needed it, that the sooner he left, the better.

He took her laptop, warm fingers brushing hers. Such a simple, caring gesture, yet it made her realise how rare it was. She had no one special in her life except her brother and father, and they were away for the rest of the year. Her father somewhere in the outback, her brother doing scientific research.

Lola beat down unfamiliar self-pity. She was *not* lonely. She was stronger than that.

'I'll organise some defensive training for you.' Niall's deep voice pulled her from her thoughts.

His company was renowned for its cyber security work but also provided everything from protection of premises to bodyguards for VIPs. It was rumoured that some of the most high-profile people in the world chose Pedersen Security.

'Thank you. That's very thoughtful.'

His dark gaze slanted down, capturing hers.

Something ricocheted through her, pulsing deep in her body and down her legs, making her knees tremble.

Niall's expression was unreadable. It wasn't the

look of a man who viewed her as an annoying responsibility. Nor was it kind.

There was nothing soft about that intent stare. It seared, sharp enough to slice through a lifetime's defences.

Lola's breath snared as that strange sensation pulsed again, drying her mouth yet turning her insides liquid. She was aware, too aware, of how close they stood.

If she lifted her hand she'd touch wool and the hard chest she'd been fantasising about since early this morning. That was when she'd seen him bare-chested and wearing only low-slung track pants as he returned from a workout in the hotel gym. She'd been transfixed by his flagrant masculinity, the beauty of that powerful body, sheened with sweat, the play of muscles as he prowled into the suite, like a conqueror arrogantly claiming the space as his.

Her fingers twitched, the pads of her fingers prickling as if she'd actually touched him.

'Shall we?'

Lola's brain blanked. Shall we what? She was stuck on the image of him, half naked and potently desirable.

Then he nodded towards the car and flicked the umbrella open and over her head.

Of course, the car.

Her tongue stuck to the roof of her mouth and she could only hope it hadn't been hanging out as she drooled.

Ignoring the heat scorching her cheeks, she hurried to the vehicle, scrambling in before he could open the door. Seconds later he'd stowed her laptop and slid into the driver's seat.

Now she was cocooned with him, the drumming rain on the roof reinforcing the sense of being cut off from the world, alone with Niall.

Lola breathed deep, centring her thoughts, and discovered the tang of damp male flesh, cedar and spice. It was intoxicating.

'If you drop me at the station I'll catch a train. Oh, and I'll need my keys.' She'd left him in charge of her flat this morning, closing up after the police.

'You don't want public transport on a night like this. Especially with Braithwaite out there somewhere. I'll take you door to door.' Niall's voice was sharp.

Had she annoyed him? Reluctantly she turned and saw his honed features were grim.

Because she'd tried to save him a trip to the suburbs?

He turned on the ignition, the powerful car growling under his touch, then swung into the street. Lola snuggled back in her seat. 'Thanks, Niall. I appreciate you helping me out. I know you're a very busy man.'

Clearly he valued his friendship with Ed enormously. Niall was a high-flyer whose time really was money.

'How do you feel about not going back to the flat tonight?'

The words took her by surprise. Yet they resonated. She'd been thinking of her return home with dread. It was her safe place but now, despite the new security arrangements, it didn't feel safe.

Lola's head swung round. 'What are you suggesting?'

Not another night in his penthouse suite. It had been what she'd needed last night, when Braithwaite's intrusion sent her hurtling into fear. But sharing that intimate space with Niall brought its own problems.

'It's the weekend. What about a little time away from the city to get some fresh air and relax? Somewhere private. After what you've been through it would do you good to unwind. You could regroup and gather your strength.'

'It sounds lovely,' she admitted. 'But it's Friday night. Places within a reasonable distance of the city will already be booked.'

'No problem. I know a place. Private and comfortable, with glorious views over the coast. I can take you.'

She frowned. 'I thought you were wrapping up your business in Melbourne today?'

'I am. That doesn't mean I can't give you a lift. And don't worry about the return trip, that's easily sorted.'

'By the coast, you say?' Lola tried not to get excited and failed. There was something about sea views that always made her feel good. Walking on the beach would help her unwind. 'Is it very expensive?'

In the gloom she caught the flash of his smile. 'Mate's rates. I have an in with the owner so it's free.'

'I couldn't invite myself to stay at someone's place without—'

'It's no problem, Lola, believe me. The place is empty and the owner is more than happy for you to use it.'

She digested that. Putting off the return to her flat might make it even more difficult to go back. She needed to return soon, like getting back on a horse after being thrown, before the fear could build.

The trouble was she'd lived with fear so long her nerves were shot. If she went home she knew she'd spend the night listening for an intruder.

Her limbs ached with tiredness and too much stress. All day she'd struggled to concentrate, her mind constantly darting back to the flat, to Braithwaite, the police interview and, inevitably, to Niall. It had taken her longer than usual to complete the most ordinary tasks to her usual standard.

'I'd have to go home and pack a bag.'

He shook his head. 'I have it with me.'

Lola frowned. Hadn't she taken her overnight bag back home this morning? Or had she inadvertently left it in his hire car? She'd been so tense, returning to the flat and talking to the police, she couldn't recall.

She opened her mouth and found herself smothering a yawn. She'd been going to say she might need other things, but would she? There was a pair of jeans in there with a shirt and pullover, comfy pyjamas and toiletries. She imagined herself curled up on a sofa looking down over the sea and felt the tightness in her shoulders ease.

It was unorthodox, going away on the spur of the moment. Lola planned everything carefully.

But where was the harm in doing something on impulse for once? She could trust Niall's judgement. It would be somewhere safe and comfortable and she could pay him back for the return travel costs.

'I…okay. Thank you. That sounds perfect.'

He nodded and in the light from an oncoming car she saw him smile.

'It does, doesn't it? Why don't you close your eyes and rest?'

Lola didn't shut her eyes but she did zone out a little, relaxing to the swish of water on the road and the rhythmic beat of windscreen wipers. Instead of focusing on the city streets she surreptitiously watched Niall's strong hands on the wheel. His movements were economical and she felt safe with him.

Anxiety was still there, gnawing beneath the surface, but not that terrible panic she'd fought, discovering her home had been invaded.

Which led her inexorably back to Braithwaite. To the police assurance that they'd question him about breaking into her flat. Yet she didn't hold out much hope that they'd prove he was responsible.

Would this go the same way as when he'd stalked Therese? Would they only be able to prove something when he attacked her?

Lola shivered and sat straighter, rubbing her arms, trying to dispel a chill that settled despite the car's warm air.

She looked out and it took a while to recognise their surroundings.

'This isn't the way to the coast!'

'It is when we're flying.'

Lola goggled as Niall took an exit off the highway. 'Flying?' He couldn't be serious.

'Better than driving in this weather. It's only a short trip.'

The rain was even heavier now, pounding down and turning nearby lights into starbursts.

'I'm not flying anywhere!' She whipped around. It was one thing to agree to a coastal retreat. But this—

'You have something against planes? Are you a nervous flyer?'

'No. I like flying.' She'd only done it twice, flying to Sydney and back. She'd loved it. The bustle of the airport, the sense of expectation, the thrust of the engines accelerating as the plane rose. And the views. It had been wonderful, watching the world spread beneath her.

It had felt like adventure. For the first time in her life she'd allowed herself to feel jealous of Ed, heading off to far-flung places. He'd been away from home when their world imploded and it had been left to her to deal with their father's descent into grief. Since then she'd been tied to Melbourne, building her career, supporting her father and saving for the future. But one day…

'I can't fly away for the weekend on the spur of the moment.'

'Why not, when I can give you a lift?' Niall nosed the car through tall gates and she realised they were on the edge of an airfield. 'I'm going that way and can arrange for your return.'

He made it sound like a stop on a bus route! Then the headlights revealed what she guessed was a private jet.

Again it struck her how vastly separate Niall's world was from hers. All that linked them were a few shared years in the past, her brother Ed and a sexual pull that was totally one-sided. She was an ordinary working girl while he featured on rich lists and sexiest bachelor lists. He attended glamorous events and thought nothing of travelling by private jet.

He stopped the car and turned, gathering both her hands in his before she guessed his intentions.

His hands were large and reassuring. It would be so easy to relax under his touch. Too easy.

Or to imagine those long fingers moving across her body.

'Come on, Lola. It will be fun. A break away, time to recharge the batteries. You don't have to do a thing. What's holding you back?'

The feeling she was being railroaded.

Niall was making plans for her as if he knew best, when Lola had been taking care of herself and her dad since she was almost sixteen. She wasn't used to ceding control.

The fact that it meant spending more time with Niall.

Something curled low in her body and she knew that was part of it. No matter what she tried to tell herself, her attraction to Niall Pederson hadn't waned and she knew she shouldn't feed it.

His thumb stroked the back of her hand, sending a tingle all the way up her arm then down to her breasts.

'Ed's worried about you. He'd be relieved to know you're having a break.'

'You haven't told him—?'

'Not yet, though I don't see why you haven't.'

Lola shrugged. 'There isn't anything he could do where he is and he'd just worry.'

Niall shook his head, his expression sombre. 'It's what big brothers do. Or they should.' His voice dipped low on a note she didn't recognise and all trace of a smile disappeared. She felt him stiffen, his fingers tightening.

Was he worried about Ed taking him to task if she went back home when Niall left?

She thought of all he'd done for her in the last twenty-four hours.

But that wasn't why she was tempted to say yes. She wanted what he offered.

'Okay. I'll tell Ed about it all.' She paused then made up her mind. Her hesitation was out of proportion with the situation. 'And, yes, I'll accept the offer of a coastal escape. Thank you.'

As the plane began its descent, Niall looked at the woman asleep in the chair beside him and told himself he was doing the right thing.

Yet alarm signals chimed in his brain.

Not because he was taking drastic measures to protect Lola. He'd do whatever it took to keep her safe. That was a given. He knew what it was to lose someone important. He'd never allow that to happen again.

The alarms jangled because of what he felt. The way his gaze clung to her mouth and those high breasts that would fit perfectly in his palms. The directions his imagination roved whenever he was with her.

And even when he wasn't.

This morning's session at the gym had been prompted by images of her looking ridiculously sexy in flannel pyjamas and an oversized robe. His workout had been rigorous to the point of punishing and he'd congratulated himself on mastering his wayward libido. Till he'd entered the suite and there she'd been, tousled curls loose around her shoulders, her cute pyjamas drawing attention to all that lithe femininity despite the fact she was covered from neck to ankle.

He swallowed some coffee, difficult over the constriction in his throat.

This was wrong. Lola was like family, or should be. Ed would have his hide if he touched her. The Suarez family trusted him. She was vulnerable and he had no business lusting after her. His duty was to concentrate on keeping her safe.

If those weren't reasons enough to keep his distance, there was the darkness inside him. The darkness of grief and grim self-knowledge.

Niall knew, had known most of his life, that he could never offer the things a woman like Lola deserved. He couldn't do long term or play happy families. The very thought brought on spiralling panic. He looked down and deliberately unfolded his fists, seeking calm.

There were women in his life—he wasn't into self-denial—but there'd never be a wife or long-term partner. Absolutely no children.

He needed, deserved to be alone.

He swallowed the last of his coffee, only to find

it bitter and cold. The steward took it from him and advised they'd land soon.

Niall looked again at Lola, her face pale. She seemed younger in sleep, reminding him of their age gap and their divide in experience and character.

She was cautious yet determined, capable and feisty. And sexy. Far sexier than Ed's little sister should be. While he…

Niall slammed a steel door down. No point thinking about it. His priority was keeping her safe. End of story.

To his amazement she slept through landing and was still asleep when it was time to disembark.

How long had she been fretting over Braithwaite? Niall's chest tightened, realising she probably slept from sheer exhaustion. Helped perhaps by the glass of wine she'd accepted after they took off.

He could wake her, but he hadn't the heart. Instead he lifted her into his arms and grimaced.

Because she felt too good. She sank against him and his body seemed to sigh in relief. His tight throat turned desert dry as he strove and failed not to catalogue every centimetre of delicious femininity snuggled against him.

She murmured something as he took her to his waiting car. But instead of waking she just curled closer, so trusting that a sliver of ice spiked his heated awareness.

She spoke again, something he couldn't make out, probably because he was transfixed by the movement of her lips against his neck, her humid breath an unintentional caress that shot straight to his libido.

Settling her in the car and fixing her seat belt was a form of torture Niall had never experienced. No matter how he tried, he came into contact with things he shouldn't. The whisper slide of nylon-clad legs against his palms. Her slim waist, the gentle flare of her hips. A strand of hair caught his shirt button and it took too long to disengage himself. Doing up her seat belt, he brushed her breast with his knuckle and his groin tightened.

Instantly he straightened, the pain as his head collided with the car almost welcome.

Finally, they were on their way. It was good to have traffic and gear changes to distract him. They left the city behind and he swung the car onto the road that led into the hinterland mountains.

They were almost there when a husky voice broke the silence. 'Where are we?'

Lola shifted in her seat, turning towards the view of lights glittering along the coast below.

'That's not Melbourne. It's not familiar at all.' Her voice was sharper and she sat straighter. 'Niall?'

He tightened his grip on the wheel.

How would Lola react when she discovered he'd kidnapped her?

CHAPTER FOUR

'QUEENSLAND. THAT'S THE Gold Coast down there.'

Lola shook her head. But this wasn't like clearing blocked ears after a swim. She'd heard Niall's words. She just couldn't believe them.

One swift look at his profile in the dashboard lights revealed he appeared the same as ever. He wasn't joking. There was no sign of humour on that strong, handsome profile. He looked arrogantly sure of himself.

'Queensland?' She tested the word on her tongue, yet it didn't seem possible.

Lola swivelled back to the view down the mountain, now partially obscured as they passed through forest.

There was no mistaking the vista for Melbourne or its surrounds. There was a long, lighted urban strip with a cluster of high-rise buildings and network of streets. It trailed, like a string of glittering jewels, into the distance. Beyond it was the immense darkness of the sea. The Pacific Ocean if Niall told the truth.

Why would he lie?

'That's ridiculous! It's two states away from Victoria! Queensland is thousands of kilometres away.'

'About one thousand three hundred from Melbourne. Only a couple of hours by plane.'

'Only!' She clutched the arm rest on the door, her breath coming in shallow pants. 'This isn't what we discussed.'

Her head reeled. Again she looked out of the window but the view was the same. Stunning but unfamiliar.

How could she not have known?

How could she have slept through it all?

Because you've been running on empty for weeks. Stress at home. The new challenge at work. Juggling too much and not sleeping for fear of what Braithwaite would do next.

'I invited you to get away somewhere quiet and safe. That's where we're going.'

He sounded maddeningly calm.

Lola wanted to screech that he'd tricked her. That he had no right to do it. Instead she fought for calm, desperately sucking in a deep breath that still didn't fill her lungs. She dug her fingers into the leather of her seat. It was softer than any car upholstery she'd known. Niall swung around a rising bend and it registered that the car sat low to the ground. Some sort of sports car?

For some obscure reason the idea infuriated her.

Niall with his private plane and his expensive car, walking in and taking over her life.

'Don't play that game with me,' she snarled. 'You deliberately misled me.' She swallowed, realising with shock that unfamiliar tears clogged her throat. She'd *trusted* Niall. Now she felt as if he'd made a fool of her. 'You *manipulated* me!'

That got his attention. His head snapped round and he finally looked directly at her. She stared back, furious and wounded.

He turned to the road, slowing for a bend. 'It was for your own good.'

Her hackles rose. His tone was that of an adult reining in impatience at childish behaviour.

She wasn't a child to be pacified with platitudes. Especially over something so important.

'What paternalistic claptrap! It may have passed your notice, Niall, but I'm an adult. *I* decide what's for my own good. Not you.'

'I *had* noticed. The change in you is hard to miss.' His voice ground low in a way that burred through her insides. That only added to her ire. She was furious yet he'd managed to make her aware of him in the visceral way a woman was aware of a virile man. 'Would you have come if I'd told you?'

'Of course not.'

'You've just made my point.' His voice hardened.

'Stop the car.'

'Sorry?'

'Stop the car. I need to get out.'

'Are you sick?' The arrogant so and so had the nerve to sound concerned. Maybe he didn't like the idea of her damaging his precious sports car.

It was on the tip of her tongue to say *yes, sick of you*, but she wasn't that juvenile. She knew he'd acted out of protectiveness, but she was a grown woman who made her own decisions.

She was honest enough to know part of her distress came from the fact he saw her not as a woman in her own right but an obligation, a responsibility to be organised as a favour to his friend Ed.

The car slowed and she waited for it to stop. Instead it turned off the road onto a curving private drive. Finally it halted before an elegant entrance, lit by glowing lamps.

Lola wrestled her seat belt undone and turned to open her door, only to discover it was already open, lifting up in an unfamiliar way she'd only seen in films. She shot to her feet, reeling a moment as she felt the warm road surface beneath stockinged feet. She'd lost her shoes somewhere but right now didn't care. All she cared about was putting some distance between herself and that conniving, lying—

'Lola.' His voice came from just behind her. 'Are you ill?' Hard fingers grasped her elbow till she yanked free, spinning to face him.

'Don't you dare touch me!' Her chest rose and fell rapidly and her pulse thundered in her ears.

'You need to calm down.'

Again that oh-so-patient and utterly infuriating tone.

She shoved her hands onto her hips and met his dark gaze with a fulminating glare. 'If you say I'm overreacting I really *will* lose my temper.' Childish it might be but there'd be a lot of satisfaction to be gained in slapping that confident face. 'What makes you think you've got the right to take over my life and make decisions for me?'

To her chagrin her voice wobbled and she bit down hard on her bottom lip.

Everything felt so alien. Not just the balmy, humid air caressing her overheated cheeks, or the lush, sweet perfume of night-flowering plants. This sudden uprush of strong emotion was alien to Lola. This feeling of being adrift, at someone else's mercy, when she'd spent so many years keeping her feet firmly on the ground, achieving her goals through hard work, planning and perseverance.

It made her wobbly inside to discover she was no longer in control of her world.

It had nothing to do with the intense, disturbing effect Niall Pederson had on her.

'I'm only keeping you safe and—'

'No.' She dropped her voice to the low, authoritative pitch she'd learned projected well in meetings. 'You did a lot more.' She paused, breathing down the debilitating mix of shock, helplessness and incandescent fury. 'I've already got one crackpot in

Melbourne obsessively trying to control me and now I've got you, a man I trusted, doing the same.'

She saw that strike home. Niall's head jerked back as if she'd hit him. The flesh across his high cheekbones drew taut and even in this light she saw colour streak across his features.

'You can't compare me to that bastard!'

Lola didn't bother to answer, she turned back to the car, fumbling on the floor for her shoes and putting them on. Logic told her it was an unfair comparison, but what Niall had done was unfair too. *Duping* her!

'Where's my purse?'

'You won't need it.'

'Sorry?' She swung around and took a step closer.

He folded his arms across his solid chest. He looked utterly implacable. 'You won't need money here. You're my guest.'

'*Your* guest.' She should have known. 'This is your place?'

He shrugged. 'I live in Brisbane. I bought this as a retreat but so far I haven't had time to retreat much.'

'So you lied about having an in with the owner. You made me think it was some friend.'

Niall moved his head from one side to the other as if trying to relieve a stiff neck. Yet he stood solidly before her, as if nothing so insignificant as her preferences would move him.

'I thought I'd short-circuit exactly the sort of argument we're having now.' He paused, his expression stern. 'Come inside and make yourself comfortable, Lola. It's late and you're tired.'

She shook her head. 'I want my luggage and my purse. I'll phone for a taxi.'

Again Niall tilted his head, his eyes narrowing. Did he move a fraction closer? 'There aren't taxis that come so far.'

'There must be someone who can drive me.' She lifted her chin, refusing to give up.

'I can't think who. One of the beauties of this place is its isolation. Which makes it perfect as an escape from your Mr Braithwaite. I doubt he's got the resources to follow us here, even if he could find out where you are.'

She clenched her teeth. He wasn't *her* Mr Braithwaite. Then, reading the expression on Niall's face, she wondered if he'd deliberately said that to distract her and divert her anger.

Lola looked up the long driveway, remembering how isolated the road had seemed. Perhaps there were neighbours further along but did she want to try finding out so late at night?

The cleansing surge of molten fury vied with innate pragmatism. She'd love to see Niall's face if she stomped off into the night. But then she'd be lost and alone with no money and no phone. And, knowing Niall, she wouldn't be alone for long. He was strong enough and ruthless enough to follow, toss her over his shoulder and carry her inside.

She quivered at the image that created in her whirling brain. That annoyed her too.

Swallowing her anger, she turned and marched towards the entrance of what she saw now was a magnificent house. 'I'll leave you to bring in the luggage.' And he'd better bring her phone and purse or she'd kick up such a rumpus he wouldn't know what hit him.

Niall must have unlocked the front door remotely. It was oversized, intricately carved timber in the Balinese style, finished with touches of gilding. On either side massive brass pots held glossy, broad-leaved plants that looked lush and exotic.

If the warm night hadn't alerted her that she was far from Melbourne, these tropical touches would.

The door opened easily and she found herself in an airy foyer with a soaring ceiling and polished wooden floor that led to a massive lounge. Beyond that were full-length windows that framed the starry strip of coastal lights.

Lola took off her high heels and padded across the floor. From what she could see, the place was magnificent and built on a grand scale, but with a relaxed vibe that made her think of tropical comfort and abundance.

The impression intensified as she flicked on a switch and saw sprawling lounges, beautiful fans suspended from the double-height ceiling and a display of exquisite orchids, not in tiny indoor pots, but in a glassed atrium open to the sky.

It was all sumptuous and inviting, each detail beautiful in itself and adding to a harmonious whole.

Another light, another sitting room, a glimpse of an enormous state-of-the-art kitchen, but it was the view that drew her. Even though her thoughts should be on planning to get out of here.

Maybe, she mused, pausing before sliding glass doors that led onto a wide deck, she was drawn to the view because it was easier than thinking of mundane practicalities. Of returning to cold, wet Melbourne and the threat of Braithwaite.

She shivered and crossed her arms.

Niall's right. This would be a perfect place to unwind.

Was it weak to want to hide from what awaited her at home instead of facing it?

What she hadn't realised was that the house sat high at the top of a slope. Below her she saw the inky darkness of treetops and beyond that the coastal development, glittering gemlike in the velvet night.

As she stood there, surrounded by silence, drinking in that amazing view, Lola's jangling emotions eased. It went against the grain to admit it but, though she loathed his arrogant actions, she could appreciate Niall's attempt to help.

Except he'd treated her like a package to be delivered or a child to be coaxed.

'Would you like supper? We only had a snack on the plane.' Niall's deep voice came from behind her.

She'd been so caught up in her thoughts she hadn't heard him approach.

Lola huffed in wry amusement. Her idea of a snack was an apple. On their private flight they'd had blinis with smoked salmon and caviar then delicious hot savoury pastries. How the other half lived!

'I'm fine.' Even if she were hungry, she wasn't ready to share supper with this man.

Lola turned and sucked in a sharp breath.

For it hit her that she was totally alone with Niall Pedersen, the man who'd haunted her dreams for years.

This wasn't like last night in a busy city hotel. She was in his house and they were utterly alone. There was no housekeeper bustling out to welcome them.

Something about the still darkness and the lush, almost decadent luxury of this place made her hyper aware of Niall the man. Not the billionaire or family friend or would-be protector or even the outrageous kidnapper.

Warm light spilled across black hair that she knew from childhood games was soft and thick. He stood with his back to the light, so his eyes were shadowed, but there was no mistaking the strong shape of his jaw and nose or the lines of his mouth.

Her gaze flicked there and a mariachi band started up deep inside. No, not mariachi, the beat was sultry and compelling. It was a salsa. Or a tango.

Lola swallowed and fixed on a point past one wide shoulder.

'I'm not hungry.' Nor was she up to arguing with him. Despite sleeping through most of the journey, Lola felt incredibly weary. She needed her wits about her to deal with Niall. 'If you'll show me my room, I'd like some privacy.'

His head jerked up as if she'd surprised him.

Or disappointed him.

She had no idea where the idea came from. It wasn't as if he wanted her company and he couldn't expect her to want his after his high-handed actions.

If he wanted thanks, he'd get that from Ed, who probably wouldn't object to his ruthless methods.

'This way.' Niall spun on his heel and led her down a long corridor subtly illuminated with up-lights.

Lola followed, trying to work out what it was about his body language that told her he was tense. When she'd argued with him it had been like water off a duck's back, he'd been so convinced he was right.

He'd pushed up the sleeves of his shirt and his strong, sinewed forearms swung with each step. He moved easily, long legs eating up the space, yet somehow she knew he wasn't as relaxed as he seemed.

He pushed open a door and gestured her inside.

If she'd thought the rest of the house the epitome of tropical luxury, it paled before this.

Lola couldn't stifle a gasp. One wall was all windows, giving out onto that coastal view. The rest of the room, lit by the glow of small lamps, was an exotic paradise. A huge four-poster bed dominated one end, sheer curtains draping it. Its headboard was another huge gilded Balinese carving, this time of birds and flowers. Another wall consisted of an enormous mural of peacocks, shimmering in the warm light. There were comfortable chairs, occasional tables and pots of brightly flowering plants she didn't recognise.

'Your bathroom and dressing room are through there. That's where I left your cases.'

She swung around. 'Cases? There's only the overnight bag and laptop.'

He shrugged. 'You weren't prepared for a trip to Queensland so I took the liberty of packing suitable clothes before I left the flat. You won't want winter clothes here.'

Lola opened her mouth and shut it. She spun away towards the window but what caught her attention wasn't the view but Niall's reflection, watching her with the intensity of a hawk. His hands hung loose at his sides, fingers flexing as if anticipating trouble.

No wonder!

She swung back, narrowing her eyes on that handsome, imperious face.

'You went through my *things*?' She imagined him rifling through her clothes, her sensible work outfits and her casual jeans and shirts. Had he plundered her underwear drawer too?

Heat seared her throat and cheeks at the idea of Niall's hand touching her underwear.

That's as close as you'll ever get to that particular fantasy. The only way he'd touch your undies is if you're not in them.

Because he's not and never has been interested in you.

She'd understood that for years. Yet still it hurt.

Because no other man had toppled Niall Pedersen from the pinnacle where her infatuation had placed him. No other guy had been as caring, as strong yet funny, as spectacularly macho yet considerate, as downright attractive as the guy who'd hung around her home in those formative years. Even now, furious and hurt, she couldn't think of a man who made her hormones sit up and beg the way he did.

Lola's pride smarted. Had he noticed the difference between her cheap, chain-store clothes and the expensive designer fashions his girlfriends wore? Had he felt sorry for her? Thought her less feminine because her underwear wasn't expensive silk and lace but cotton?

'Jayden Braithwaite could learn from you, Niall.' The words emerged husky with pain. 'He might have got into my home but as far as I know he hasn't yet stooped low enough to paw through my underwear.'

Niall flinched, head snapping back as her words lashed him.

She couldn't *really* compare him to the man stalking her! She *knew* Niall acted out of care for her.

Yet he couldn't miss her convulsive swallow or the scratchy, thickened sound of her voice as if she battled tears.

The Lola he knew hated crying, saw it as a sign of weakness. Even the day of her mother's funeral, she'd pulled away from him and not let the tears fall, though she'd adored her mother and he knew her heart was breaking.

His own throat tightened, her emotion stirring something visceral.

Niall told himself she was overreacting, trying to make him feel bad because she preferred to manage her own life—

But that's the point, Pedersen.

She's a woman, not a kid. You know that.

She's capable and strong. She didn't ask you to come in and push her into a solution of your own making, even if it's what you and Ed would prefer.

Niall tried to imagine sitting back while someone else directed his life. Tried and failed.

'I'm sorry, Lola.'

Her eyebrows rose but her mouth remained a taut, flat line that told him she didn't believe his apology.

'I keep forgetting you're not...'

'What? A kid who hero-worshipped you?'

'Hero worship?' He snorted. 'You might have tagged along with me and Ed but, as I recall, you were pretty good at holding your own.'

'And I prefer to do that now.' Bitterness laced her

tone and her chin jutted high. Somehow she managed to look down her nose at him, though without her shoes she barely reached his shoulder.

'Again, I apologise. I wasn't thinking of anything but getting you somewhere safe. If you'd been any other woman...' Of course he'd have baulked at sorting out her clothes and especially her underwear. He took a slow breath. 'You and Ed are like family, so I just acted. But it *was* an invasion of your privacy.'

His apology was honest as far as it went. Yet if he were totally truthful, there was a moment when he'd grabbed a handful of her underwear, intending to pack it, and stopped. The feel of the soft cotton had made him wonder how it would be to touch Lola's glorious body through it.

Would she look cute and demure wearing the white bra with its tiny red bow and the bikini panties sprigged with clusters of cherries? Or would she be unbearably sexy, so irresistible he'd lose his battle to ignore the fact she'd turned into a siren?

He'd held her in his arms after they discovered Braithwaite had been in her home and, along with the desire to comfort her, Niall had felt another sort of desire. One that shamed him. For, even if they weren't blood relations, Niall and the Suarez family viewed him as an honorary family member.

Yet the surge of lust was real. And it was back with a vengeance.

Heat rose from the pit of his belly and his hairline prickled damply, his palms turning clammy.

Was she wearing another demure white bra? Panties dotted with strawberries this time?

His fingers twitched and his palm tingled as, unbidden, that question again filled his brain. How would it feel, touching that soft cotton when it was taut across Lola's gentle curves? He remembered the sway of her hips and beautiful backside in that pencil skirt and the memory was a grinding weight in his groin, turning and twisting.

Little Lola had changed all right. She'd become the sort of woman a man could lose his mind over. And she wasn't even trying!

She stared at him as if unimpressed by his apology. But even with a frown and her arms crossed impatiently, Lola Suarez affected him as no woman had in as long as he could remember.

Her pulse, the delicate flutter at the base of her throat, seemed like an invitation to a man who, after a sleepless night imagining her delicious body just metres away, was too close to the edge. How would she taste there? Sweet or salty? How about her lips? Her breasts, her...

'I'll be just down the hall.' His voice emerged gruff and abrupt. 'Call me if you need anything.' Then he turned and strode from the room.

Because, he realised suddenly, being here alone with Lola was the worst idea he'd ever had.

For as well as needing to protect her, Niall had one other need. One that was wholly inappropriate. To seduce Lola Suarez. To ravish her thoroughly, again and again and again, until he rid himself of this burning hunger.

CHAPTER FIVE

IT WAS HARD to stay angry after the best night's sleep she'd had in ages. Whether from exhaustion or the fact she was out of Braithwaite's reach, Lola had sunk onto that flagrantly romantic bed and been asleep before she had time to think.

For that she had Niall to thank. At home she'd have tossed and turned, on edge and sleepless.

While she fumed at his autocratic, take-charge attitude, she understood he'd done what he had because he cared.

Just not in the way she wanted.

If you'd been any other woman, he'd said. Which explained everything.

He didn't think of her as a woman, much less a desirable one. To him she was Ed's kid sister, part of the Suarez family that had informally adopted him.

He cared for her like a sister.

Lola stifled a grimace and, pulling on a summery print dress, and trying not to think of Niall's hands on it, left her room. She didn't straighten her hair or put it up as she did for the office. Nor did she put on make-up. She refused to primp for a man who thought she had the sex appeal of a piece of furniture. And she didn't need make-up to boost her confidence.

She had this. She'd be polite but firm. She'd organise a return flight to Melbourne and she'd—

Lola stopped in the kitchen doorway, all thought of grabbing toast and tea disintegrating.

Her pulse beat high in her throat as she took in Niall, hair damp and a thin T-shirt clinging to a wall of muscle. He might have just walked out of the surf with a board under his arm, but he'd probably just emerged from the shower. He looked tanned, taut and terrific and her stomach did a belly flop at the sight.

'You're up. Great. Ready for breakfast?'

His smile was easy but she saw wariness in his eyes. He was wondering what sort of mood she was in. No wonder, in all the time they'd known each other she'd never before lost her temper with him.

'I am. I'm starving.' Her gaze roved the food spread on the massive island bench. 'Are you cooking?'

Better to concentrate on food than on the fact Niall looked good enough to eat. She wasn't going to notice that any more. After she left here she doubted she'd see him again for another eight years.

'Absolutely, if you want something hot. Otherwise we've got tropical fruit, muffins, fresh pastries from the best patisserie on the coast, thick Greek yoghurt with honey and nuts—'

'That's more than enough!' She approached the array of food. 'You've been out to a patisserie?'

He shook his head. 'My housekeeper dropped them off. Her husband is a pastry chef.' At her querying look he added, 'They live further along the mountain. Now, coffee, juice, tea or maybe a Mimosa?'

'A Mimosa?'

Niall opened a massive fridge and produced a foil-topped bottle. 'Champagne and freshly squeezed orange juice. Not recommended on a workday, but I thought you might like to celebrate being on holiday.'

'I'd hardly call it a holiday.'

Niall shrugged and loaded a wicker basket of pastries onto a vast tray along with a colourful selection of tropical fruit. 'You're not working and it's a glorious day. Why not relax and enjoy it? Ed tells me you haven't taken a holiday in ages.'

He did, did he? Lola's eyebrows twitched into a frown. What else had Ed told him?

Then she looked in the direction of Niall's outstretched arm towards the broad deck and her annoyance died. The view of rainforest, sea and city was even more magnificent in daylight. One end of the deck was taken up with a sparkling infinity pool where light danced on crystal water. As she watched, a flock of birds with iridescent plumage, lime green, blue, red and orange, darted across to a nearby tree, so stunningly bright they didn't look real.

'Rainbow Lorikeets,' Niall murmured. 'If we sit outside we can watch them.'

For a moment Lola hesitated. But she was no fool. How often did she get the chance to enjoy such surroundings? Her time here was limited so she'd make the most of it.

'Yes, please, to eating outside.' Her gaze strayed to the wine bottle; she was about to ask for plain juice when something stopped her. 'And yes to the Mimosa.'

She'd never had champagne at breakfast. It felt daring and decadent.

Her life was devoid of extravagance as she worked to build her career and her savings to afford her own place. Certainty and safety were important to her.

That was why there'd been no holidays away and no fripperies. Why her life was, in many ways, empty of excitement. But Lola wasn't going to look a gift horse in the mouth. She'd enjoy this while she could. In a couple of hours she'd probably be boarding a sardine-packed economy flight to Melbourne.

The temperature outside was balmy compared with the icy rain they'd left behind. Was it the warmth that made her relax, or the stunning surroundings, high on this mountain surrounded by birdsong and the fragrance of blossoms?

Even her interaction with Niall was different. Neither mentioned their reason for being here or their argument. Instead they chatted casually, as if the years had telescoped and they were still in the habit of sharing a table, not needing to fill every silence.

Finally, Lola leaned back and sipped her drink. The tang of fresh juice and the tingle of bubbles made her smile. It really did make the meal a special occasion.

In other circumstances she'd love to stay here. But she had to reclaim her life.

'I slept late. I haven't had a chance to look at return flights. Do you know when they leave?'

Niall put down his glass, his face suddenly serious.

'I don't think that's a good idea.'

'Nevertheless, I need to organise a flight.' She kept her voice even. Last night she'd been furious but she wasn't making that error again. She didn't like scenes and hated losing control. All she had to do was treat Niall like a colleague. As if he didn't get under her skin.

'Lola...'

It was unlike Niall to hesitate. Plus there was something about the gruff note in his voice that made her do what she'd avoided all through the meal. She looked directly into his eyes.

What she saw made her breath hitch. His navy gaze was intent and sombre. With his knotted brow and grimly set jaw, he looked like the bearer of bad tidings. Or a man about to try to change her mind.

'I know you're concerned for me, Niall, and I appreciate it. You were wonderful, looking after me on Thursday when I needed it—I can't thank you enough for that. And this getaway...' she shrugged. 'I know you planned it with the best intentions. But I need to get back.'

Not because she really wanted to be in her flat but because it would be a mistake staying here under the same roof with him.

She might have slept the night through but she vividly remembered fragments of her dreams and they frightened her. She didn't dream of Braithwaite. Instead, it was Niall who'd featured in her imaginings, Niall, bare-chested, his hard hands skimming all over her body, making her feel...

Heat swamped her and she reached again for her glass, gulping down the cool nectar.

'There's something you don't know.'

'Sorry?' It took a moment to surface from last night's fevered imaginings. How real Niall's touch had felt as his hand dipped over her belly and down between her legs while he lowered his head to her breast and sucked her nipple.

'I didn't tell you everything in Melbourne.'

She blinked. 'What do you mean? What's wrong?' She tried and failed to imagine what he might have withheld. Horror widened her eyes and she leaned closer. 'Is it something about Ed? Or Dad?' Her father wasn't the best at keeping in touch, especially when he was camping somewhere remote in the Northern Territory. 'Has there been an accident?'

'No! They're both okay.' Niall shook his head. 'I'm sorry to scare you. It's nothing like that.'

She slumped back, hand to her chest. Anything else she could handle. It might be almost a decade since her mother had died and Lola's world had shattered, but she remembered the devastation as if it were yesterday.

'It's about Braithwaite. He didn't just poison your plants.' He paused. 'I was about to tell you that night in your flat, but you were so upset when you discovered he'd been there. I thought it better to wait till you were calmer. But there never seemed a good time.'

Lola straightened, hands gripping the table. She remembered how desperately she'd clung to him that night. No wonder he'd hesitated before giving more bad news. 'Go on.'

'I found glass in your teapot.'

It took a moment for her to process his words. 'It's made of tempered glass.'

His mouth tightened. 'Ground glass. The pot itself wasn't damaged so it didn't come from that. It was put there deliberately.'

For a second it didn't make sense, then Lola found herself on the brink of nausea. The sunlit scene wavered as she imagined what might have happened. But it hadn't happened, because Niall had noticed and saved her. Yet horror darkened the edges of her vision.

She reached out and closed her fingers around his hand. 'Thank you. I mightn't have seen it and then—'

'Don't think about it!' His sharp voice told its own story. He appeared calm but he wasn't unmoved. His hand turned beneath hers and squeezed.

'I always knew he was dangerous, and he seemed to be getting closer and closer to me.' She just hadn't realised how close. Another wave of sickness threatened and she beat it down. It was okay to be scared but she needed to be strong. 'You told the police?'

He nodded. 'We had a long discussion.'

Lola's eyes narrowed, reading his expression. Her nape prickled in premonition. 'There's more, isn't there?'

Niall drew in a slow breath. 'I found a surveillance camera in your flat.'

'What?' She was on her feet, adrenaline shooting through her blood.

'A miniature camera in the hallway. It would give a view of the living room and the bedroom end of the hall.'

The bedroom end…

Her stomach churned at the thought of Braithwaite gloating, watching her when she didn't know. Maybe watching her undress or shower.

'Just one?'

'Yes. The police were going to go over the place with a fine-tooth comb.'

The bright blue sky dimmed and she shivered, her bare arms pimpling as if from a blast of arctic air.

Lola's mouth worked but no words formed. She stumbled away from the table then stopped.

A laugh escaped, a sharp crack of sound that held no humour but spoke of despair and shock. How long had Braithwaite spied on her? How pointless her caution and her reports to the police when he knew her every move?

'Ah, Lola.' Niall was before her, a blur seen through stinging eyes. 'Come here.'

She heard the ache of sympathy in his voice and shook her head. Better not to touch him. She felt weak enough as it was. Her whole body trembled and her knees wobbled alarmingly.

'I'm okay. Just surprised.' She lifted her chin.

But that only brought her gaze on a collision course with Niall's. His handsome features softened in sympathy as he closed the gap between them. Lola felt his heat warm her all the way down her body, but she resisted the urge to sway closer. It would be a bad idea.

A large hand slid under her hair to cup her cheek. Niall's touch was firm and sure. How she craved some of his strength and certainty.

Fearing he'd read that yearning, she let her eyelids drop, sighing. For no matter how strong she

told herself she was, she didn't have the willpower
to step back.

Lola was torn between wanting more and hating
herself for this vulnerability. So she stood, concentrating on sucking air into oxygen-starved lungs and
trying not to move closer.

Her mind should be full of fear and worry about
Braithwaite but somehow that dimmed when Niall
was near.

His thumb moved, stroking her cheek, and her
breath shuddered out.

'Lola.' His voice sounded different. Deeper.
Thicker. She felt it like a slow-moving, searing-hot
channel, carving through her insides.

Reluctantly she opened her eyes and he was
closer. If she took a deep breath surely their bodies
would brush. Instantly and, she told herself, without
intending to, she drew in just such a breath.

Her nipples stroked his hard torso and sensation
shot through her. It was electric and powerful.

His other hand grabbed her upper arm as if to
support her. But strangely, now, her knees were rock
solid. She wasn't wobbling.

Before her eyes Niall's mouth, that sculpted, sensual mouth, drew back hard as if he clenched his
teeth. Lola saw a muscle tic at the corner of his jaw.
Something about that quickened her own pulse and
her lips parted.

'Lola.' Deeper again and gruff, so unlike Niall's
usual smooth voice. She watched his Adam's apple

dip and rise in that bronzed throat and something new shuddered to life deep inside.

Lola fought it. She really did. But a lifetime's yearning wasn't easily denied.

She swallowed too, then licked her lips, her mouth dry.

'Yes, Niall.' It didn't emerge as a question, urging him to finish whatever it was he intended to say. Instead it was an affirmation. An invitation.

She heard the roughened sound of his breathing, felt the thud of his heart as she put her hand to his chest, fingers splayed, the better to absorb the feel of hard muscle and taut flesh beneath fine cotton.

She'd never touched a man that way and it felt elemental as no kiss or exploratory caress on a date ever had.

Because those guys weren't Niall.

There was something incredibly arousing about holding his heartbeat at the centre of her palm. As if he let her capture and absorb his life force.

Which was crazy. Lola was the one overcome by the need for more. Not Niall. Never Niall. He was just being kind, comforting her when she was stressed.

Yet even as she tried to convince herself she imagined things, he bowed his head lower, his breath feathering her forehead.

His hand slipped from her cheek, back into the wild waves of hair she hadn't bothered to tame. His fingers speared up her scalp, making it tingle with delicious sensation. She sank her head back against his supporting hand.

That left her face raised and open to him. Through half-closed eyes she tried to read his expression. His eyes glowed, appearing almost cobalt to her overwrought senses. His nostrils flared and his expression looked grim.

But then, instead of drawing away, he did the impossible, pulling her head back further and taking her mouth with his.

Everything stopped. Her breath, her heart, the sounds of birds in the trees. Even the whispery morning breeze seemed to die away as every nerve she possessed adjusted to his kiss.

It wasn't tentative. It wasn't a mere brush of lips across lips.

It was deliberate and sure. Like the man himself. His mouth opened over hers, his tongue sliding across her lips as of course she opened instantly for him.

After that came a dizzying, wild plunge akin to dropping off the top of a roller coaster and down the other side. Except there was no fear, only an urgent, rising delight. A hunger that had her shuffling closer, flattening her breasts against him and hooking both hands up over his shoulders.

Niall looped an arm around her waist, pulling her in as their mouths fused. It was bliss.

Lola's eyes closed. Not because she didn't want to see him, but because the sensations bombarding her demanded all her attention. Everything was heightened, her body sensitised so she felt even the slightest touch acutely.

Sparks ignited where her breasts crushed against him, his arm around her back was deliciously heavy and the things he did with his tongue... She pressed against him, meeting those druggingly deep forays into her mouth with urgent demands of her own.

No kiss had ever felt like this. So utterly right. So much more than a meeting of mouths.

Niall kissed with his whole body and she revelled in it. The hard strain of bunched muscles against her body that made her feel flagrantly feminine. The heat, that had started as a transfer from his body to hers but which now flamed from an ignition point low in her pelvis. The taste of him, unique, indefinable and addictive, filling her head with the promise of so much more.

And when he moved, dropping his encircling arm to settle his palm on her buttocks and draw her higher... Lola gasped as she came in contact with a hard ridge.

That felt so good. *He* felt so good.

Because this was *Niall*, the man she'd fixated on more than half a lifetime ago and yearned for ever since.

Lola tilted her pelvis, accentuating the contact, and was rewarded with a deep-seated growl that reverberated from his throat into their fused mouths.

Swallowing that utterly primitive sound felt even more intimate than the urgent press of their bodies.

Sizzling arousal shot through her, making everything soften, especially that sweet spot between her legs, where he'd hitched her high against his groin.

'Niall.' It was only as she heard the word that she registered the pressure of his mouth easing. His open lips brushed hers as he breathed deep, his chest pushing out against her.

Then his mouth was gone and she opened dazed eyes.

Cobalt eyes, impossibly bright, snared hers.

Her pulse thumped as something passed between them. A primal message that made her body tremble in anticipation.

Yes! At last!

She read the reflection of her own need. The wonder and the hunger that could no longer be denied.

A smile trembled on her lips as sweet tenderness vied with urgent arousal. Finally Niall recognised it too, the force binding them together. The compulsion so strong she hadn't been able to bury it or break it or batter it into submission through years of trying.

Now she didn't have to, because Niall's eyes, and his taut, eager body, revealed this was no longer a one-sided attraction.

'Niall.' Her voice was softer this time, but no less sure. Because this, the pair of them together, was meant to be. At last he realised it too.

Large hands firmed around her arms, pulling them down and holding her steady as he stepped away.

For a second, bereft of his supporting frame, she wavered, unable to balance on her feet. Till he spoke and abruptly Lola was no longer floating in bliss but back on brutal, unforgiving ground.

'I'm sorry, Lola. That was a mistake.'

CHAPTER SIX

NIALL TRIED AND failed to quell the wild hunger within him. The urgent compulsion to taste her again, haul her close and explore every part of Lola's delectable body.

Hell! Those eyes! Wide and disbelieving. No longer hazel but a saturated green with only flecks of brown.

Hungry eyes.

Wounded.

Accusing.

His gaze dropped to her lips, plump and reddened from that no-holds-barred kiss. From *him*, devouring her as if he'd never get enough of her sweet taste and yielding softness.

No, not yielding. She'd kissed him back ardently, pressing against him, turning a gesture of comfort into a frenzy of need.

A shudder passed through him. Niall told himself it was horror at what he'd done.

Yet the fact he had to fight the urge to tuck her

in against him again, devouring not just her mouth but every inch of that supple body, told its own tale.

He wanted Lola.

He *craved* her. The last couple of days had been a nightmare, trying to protect her while at the same time wanting her for himself. Every time she got close he found himself inhaling her fresh, enticing scent. His heartbeat spiked whenever she was around. Sleeping had been close to impossible the last two nights, knowing she was lying just a room away, while he burned with unfulfilled longing.

Niall had told himself he'd imagined things. That he exaggerated a natural reaction to a gorgeous woman. That the danger she was in, and their heightened emotions, confused the issue.

He wasn't confused now. He knew with every pulse of rushing blood in his body that he wanted her.

But it was wrong.

Lola was vulnerable. She was under pressure, scared by her stalker. She hadn't thought through what she was doing.

More, she was Ed's little sister. The Suarez family had opened its arms and home to him when he was a troubled teen, flirting with danger. It had never been stated aloud but it was understood that Lola would be safe with him, despite the negative reputation he'd begun to acquire. They'd trusted him and he couldn't, wouldn't betray that trust.

'I'm sorry,' he said again, wishing he meant it.

Because even knowing it was wrong, he had to shove his hands in his pockets to stop himself reaching for her.

Those huge eyes met his. Surprisingly now he couldn't read Lola's expression. It was as if she'd brought down a shutter to hide herself from him.

Niall frowned. He didn't like the notion.

Because you want to see desire in her eyes. So you have an excuse to ignore your conscience and take what you want.

'Why?' She wrapped her arms around her middle and a chunk of something hard broke off inside him at the sight of her hurting, even if her face remained calm. 'Why was it a mistake?'

She had to ask?

Niall shook his head. 'I'm your brother's best friend.'

Her mouth turned down at the corners. 'What's that got to do with you and me?'

Niall pinched the bridge of his nose, squeezing his eyes shut for a second, hoping when he opened them her lush mouth wouldn't still be in that sultry pout.

No such luck. That explained his harsh tone. 'There *is* no you and me. It was a spur of the moment impulse.' Which made a liar of him. Oh, he'd acted on impulse, but he'd been thinking about kissing Lola since two nights ago when she'd opened her door to him. 'Because I wouldn't betray Ed like that. Or your father. You're off limits.'

Her head angled to one side. By the jut of her chin he'd guess she was angry rather than hurt, except her face had paled. That made him feel about an inch tall.

The last thing he wanted was to hurt her.

'Betray? Did Ed tell you not to kiss me? Or my father?' Before he could answer she pressed on. 'Do you usually let other people tell you who you can kiss and who you can't?'

Niall swore under his breath. 'Stop trying to twist this, Lola. We both know they wouldn't like me messing with you.'

Slowly she shook her head. 'Maybe years ago when we were young. But not now. They both think the world of you.'

Niall flattened his mouth.

That's because they don't know everything about Niall Pedersen. There's one secret not even Ed knew. One that would destroy his faith in his mate.

Because when he and Ed met, it was the last thing Niall had wanted to talk about. And later he'd feared that sharing it would kill their friendship. He'd learned to hug the past close and never speak of it.

'And...' She paused, licking her lips. To his horror, that small movement tugged a white-hot wire of need straight through his groin. 'I'm all grown up, remember? I decide what men I kiss. It's no one's business but mine.'

Niall understood the point she was making but part of him was still back with her deciding what men she kissed. It was unreasonable and appalling, but he didn't want her kissing any man.

Any man but him.

He swallowed, the movement grating his throat.

How had this happened? This wasn't just inappropriate desire. It was all-consuming.

Niall had never been proprietorial about any woman, except perhaps for a brief time in his teens when hormones had triumphed over common sense. His relationships were exclusive but time-limited. Never before had he felt sick to the gut at the idea of his current lover eventually going off with someone else.

And Lola isn't even your lover!

This had to stop.

'The point is, I made a mistake. I shouldn't have kissed you, that's all that matters.'

'Even if you enjoyed it?'

Especially because he enjoyed it.

'Call it a conditioned reflex. I'm not proud of it, but holding a woman in my arms, an attractive woman…' he added as he saw her frown gather. Then he lifted his shoulders in a shrug as if it was some simple mistake. 'I just—'

'Got curious? Couldn't help yourself?' Her voice rang with something Niall couldn't identify. Outrage or hurt? She laughed, and the sound, so utterly lacking in amusement, made him shrivel inside. 'Is this like all cats looking the same colour in the dark? You're telling me that holding a woman, any woman, in your arms, would make you try your luck with her?'

Nothing could be further from the truth. Niall was nothing if not discriminating. But he didn't defend himself. Better she think that of him. It was sure to kill any hint of desire she felt.

He waited for her to slap him or shout at him. Instead Lola watched him steadily, as if cataloguing him for future reference. That stare was so coolly assessing he had to resist the urge to shuffle his feet and look away.

Her eyes had changed, the brilliant green less pronounced now. Her mouth was prim and tight, not the cupid's bow that had been an invitation to kiss.

His heart sank. He hated seeing her hiding hurt and disappointment. He hovered on the brink of saying he'd lied. That he wanted her.

But it was vital he convince Lola that was somewhere they couldn't go.

How could he protect her if he was distracted by sex?

Niall knew the consequences if he failed her. His stomach churned in a nauseating roil of regret and pain, flashes of the dark past exploding in his vision so that Lola's beautiful face blurred before him.

The cost of failure was too high. He refused to have yet another death on his hands.

That alone gave him the strength he needed.

'Trust me, Lola, this leads nowhere. What we need to concentrate on is how to keep you safe until Braithwaite's caught.'

He's lying.

She sensed it. Felt it in her bones.

Despite the years apart, she knew Niall. There was something he wasn't telling her. Some reason he changed the subject.

Unless he's just not into you.

Unless it's just as he said. One female body might be as good as another to him. You have no idea what sort of life he leads now.

Ed definitely wasn't going to tell her about his best friend's sexual activities. And who was she to judge with her vast inexperience?

Lola's heart jammed high behind her ribs as some of the fight bled out of her. Perhaps Niall really was programmed to respond sexually to any woman in his arms. Her mouth rucked up in a bitter smile. He'd only added *attractive* woman as an afterthought. Trying to spare her ego. Maybe she didn't even qualify as passably attractive in his rarefied world.

A sharp, sour tang filled her mouth.

Disappointment? Disillusionment?

She didn't stop to investigate. She did what she'd learned to do when her mother died and her world had shredded around her, focusing on one, tangible thing at a time and working out a way to deal with it.

'So you want me to stay here till Braithwaite's caught, is that it?'

Some of the rigidity eased from Niall's frame at her words.

One thing she couldn't fault him on. He really was concerned to keep her safe.

'It makes sense, doesn't it?'

Not if it meant sharing a space with Niall. Not when she wanted to shrivel up in a foetal position and nurse her bruised ego instead of talk with him as if what they'd just shared meant nothing at all.

She shook her head. 'That would only work if Braithwaite's caught soon. I can't put my life and my job on hold permanently.'

'You can work remotely for a while, can't you? Surely your manager would support you if you explained the circumstances.'

Niall was right. Her team was dedicated and hardworking but flexible too. She had a good boss and he'd support her if he could. But it could only be a short-term solution.

'Possibly,' she admitted reluctantly. 'But I can't stay here indefinitely. And until the police arrest Braithwaite, nothing's changed.'

'Call them. Talk to them about whether it's safe for you to return home.'

He looked so sure of himself, Lola guessed he'd already had such a conversation. Heat flared. Anger, she discovered, was a great antidote to sexual frustration and hurt pride.

'I'd planned to, straight after breakfast.' She glanced at her watch and nodded. 'I'll do it now.'

What followed left her feeling enervated. The good news was the case now seemed to be a police priority, something she hadn't been sure of before. The bad news was that there was no proof it had been Braithwaite in her flat. They'd searched his room in the boarding house where he lived but discovered nothing. Their best guess was that he'd monitored her from somewhere else.

Lola suggested coming home as a way of enticing him to overstep the mark, though her stomach cramped with anxiety at the thought. But the officer was against it. Particularly as Mr Pedersen had already offered an alternative plan.

Lola frowned. Surely this was between her and the police, not Niall?

It turned out he'd offered to have one of his security staff stay in her home. An experienced female operative who'd dress like Lola and return to the flat after dark with a suitcase like Lola's. The hidden camera had been disabled so Braithwaite couldn't watch the flat's interior. It was hoped he'd think the woman was Lola and make a move against her.

'But he might hurt her!' Lola protested.

There followed a long conversation about professional qualifications and experience. The extra surveillance equipment installed in the block of flats, which would give the resident and the police early warning if Braithwaite approached. The con-

certed effort to catch him red-handed in the very
near future.

'Frankly, Ms Suarez, with this very generous
offer of assistance from Mr Pedersen, it would be
a relief knowing you're safely out of harm's way.'

Lola ended the call feeling flat. It wasn't that she
wanted to catch her stalker herself. She'd be happy
never to lay eyes on the man again. But she felt...
useless. She counted her practical problem-solving
skills as her main asset. Now she felt helpless.

That was what made her feel so terrible. She'd
spent eight years doing everything she could to
avoid feeling that way again. Building a safe, certain
future, being capable, independent and in control.

That nightmare time when her mother died and
her father spun out of control still haunted her. She'd
felt rudderless, terrified of losing her dad too, and
their home. She'd been determined never to feel
that way again.

Lola shot to her feet, pacing her bedroom. What
was she thinking to resent professionals protecting
her? She was grateful.

The problem, apart from feeling adrift and hor-
ribly powerless, was being beholden to Niall. She
hated that. Hated the way that made her feel. Hated
that he felt sorry for her.

Hated the way he'd rejected her!

She felt first hot then cold at the memory of him
gently but inexorably pushing her away.

Lola wasn't an object of pity. She refused to be.

So she did the sensible thing and contacted her boss, explaining her situation and getting approval to work remotely for the next week.

Twenty minutes later, her bag over her shoulder, she went in search of Niall.

'I've got approval to work remotely for a week.'

'Excellent.'

He didn't look surprised and suspicion surfaced. But surely even take-control Niall wouldn't have interfered by contacting her employer. Lola shoved the notion aside.

'I'm going out for the day. I'll see you later.'

'Sorry?' That wiped the smug expression off his face. Was it petty of her to be pleased? She was sick of him setting limits for her, even if they were sensible. His intentions were good but when he hovered protectively it made her feel weak and vulnerable, exactly what she strived to avoid.

'There may not be taxis, but I've discovered there's a bus to the city from a couple of kilometres down the hill. If I go now I'll catch it easily. While I'm here I want to explore.'

Niall frowned. 'That's not a good idea.'

The coil of brooding antagonism in Lola's belly tightened. 'You said yourself that Braithwaite's unlikely to follow me here, even if he had any way of discovering where I am, which he doesn't.' She paused and gave him a cool smile. 'There's a return bus late in the afternoon. I'll see you around six.'

She'd only taken a couple of steps when Niall was before her, blocking her way.

'Why not stay here? Enjoy the pool and relax in the sun?'

It sounded tempting but Lola felt claustrophobic. She shook her head. 'I need to get out. For weeks I've felt hemmed in by the threat of a stalker. Now I've got away for a little, I refuse to hide here. I need to get out and enjoy my freedom.'

Especially as this freedom might only be fleeting. Niall and the police spoke confidently about catching Braithwaite and proving a case against him. But Lola knew how difficult it would be. And even with proof, how long would he be off the streets?

Maybe that was why she was so edgy.

Maybe it didn't have anything to do with Niall pushing her away after turning her inside out with that stunning kiss.

And if you believe that you've suddenly gone weak in the head.

'You're serious about this?'

'Oh, come on, Niall!' She jammed her hands onto her hips. 'I'm talking about a day on the Gold Coast. Broad daylight. Holiday makers. A little shopping, a little sightseeing. I'm perfectly capable of managing that.'

'It's not that.' He looked discomfited as if he belatedly realised he was overreacting.

'What's the problem, then? Afraid I'll sneak off and rent a car and go somewhere you don't know about?' She read surprise in his features and realised that for once she'd come up with something he hadn't anticipated. Her lips tugged up in a smile. 'Sadly, I can't because I don't have a driver's licence.'

She lived in a city with good public transport. And, when her friends were busy learning to drive, she'd been too occupied, devoting herself to saving her father from self-destruction.

'But I'm used to public transport.' She sidestepped and headed to the door.

'Wait.' Long fingers encircled her wrist. Shock ran through her. Tiny rivulets of effervescence as if her capillaries fizzed with electricity.

A scant second later Niall's hand dropped away as if burnt.

Lola swallowed. She'd swear her wrist bore the imprint of his fingers. Not because his touch bruised, but because she craved more. Yet he couldn't bear even that contact. Was he afraid his earlier rejection wasn't enough to keep her at bay?

'I'll drive you.'

Niall cursed the impulsive offer all the way down to the city. It had been bad enough last night, cocooned in the sports car with Lola from the airport, every sense on high alert. Not just because of possible external danger but because of the danger she presented to his self-control.

Today was worse. Barely an hour ago he'd held

her in his arms, ravaged her sweet mouth and gathered her luscious body close.

He wanted more.

Despite what he'd said about it being wrong.

He had a responsibility to protect Lola, not seduce her.

Tell that to your libido, Pedersen!

His body felt stretched, rigid with the force of control he had to exert. Because, instead of taking another swooping curve down the mountain, he wanted to coast off the road into a secluded lay-by and kiss her again. Find out if she really did taste as delicious as he remembered, like succulent summer fruit.

He wanted to discover if their bodies locked together as easily as he suspected they would.

'Have you told Ed?'

Her words sliced through his thoughts and the wheel wobbled in his hands.

Tell his best friend he lusted after Ed's kid sister? Not likely!

'Did you tell him about Braithwaite?'

Niall breathed out slowly. Braithwaite. Of course. 'No, I'll leave that to you.'

Lola snorted and he flicked her a sideways look. 'What's so funny?'

'The fact there's something you think I can do for myself.'

He frowned and shifted down a gear. 'If there's

something behind that pointed remark you'd better explain.'

Because his thought processes were slowed by insistent fantasies that featured Lola wearing a lot less than that button-through dress.

What on earth had possessed him to pack a dress for her with a line of buttons from top to bottom?

It was nothing short of an invitation to flick them undone. Slowly, savouring the delectable sight of her gradually revealed body. Or quickly, tearing it wide, because his patience wore thin and he couldn't wait a second more.

'I mean—' no missing the edge to her voice '—ever since you walked back into my world you've done your best to take over.' She raised a palm. 'I know it's because you care and I thank you for that. But I need to feel I've still got some agency in what happens to me.'

Niall scowled. 'I'm sorry you feel that way. It wasn't my intention to upset you.'

From the corner of his eye he saw her wave her hand. 'I know. Nevertheless, you need to remember I'm used to looking after myself. I make my own decisions. I have done for years.'

Niall nodded but kept his mouth shut. Blurting out that he was the one with security expertise wouldn't help, nor reiterating the fact that her stalker was precisely the sort of obsessive, violent man who posed the worst sort of threat to a woman.

He wanted Lola wary, not scared witless.

Which meant he'd have to give her some space, let her pretend this was a holiday. Back off a bit, even if he intended to stay hyper-vigilant.

Two deaths on his conscience was enough. There wouldn't be a third. Especially—his breath caught—especially not Lola.

So for the rest of the day he set out to lift her burden of fear and turn this into a holiday.

First the beach, for a stroll along the long flat, sandy strip. Then morning tea at an outdoor café where they could watch the passing parade. Then shopping.

But there again, Lola's bolshie independence disrupted his plans. Niall was happy, more or less, to accompany her into most of the boutiques. But she had other ideas. They were passing a store window filled with filmy, decadent nightgowns and underwear that alternated between minuscule and see-through.

Without pausing, Lola sashayed inside, he'd swear with an extra sway to her hips. Not by a single backward glance did she acknowledge she was gauging whether he'd follow, but he knew she'd gone there deliberately. Instead of pointing to a lacy, low-cut bra in the window as she spoke to the shop assistant, she made a production of touching it, her fingers skimming the crimson lace that surely wouldn't even cover her nipples when she tried it on.

Niall knew when he was beaten.

Stiff-legged, he walked across the road and ordered an espresso, his eyes never leaving the shop. He'd monitor her from here. If there was even a hint of threat he'd be at her side in seconds.

He could have followed her. In other circumstances he'd have revelled in it. But those circumstances would be when he was with a lover. Niall wasn't shy about sex or about a beautiful woman wearing erotic clothes. He might have chosen some items for her to try on. He'd definitely have asked to see her model them.

But not with Lola.

He'd been on the edge of arousal ever since that kiss. It was a wonder she hadn't noticed, except she'd been too busy keeping her nose in the air, indignant at his attempts to look after her. Then later, once they reached the Gold Coast, too wrapped up in the sights and sounds, like a kid on a once-in-a-lifetime treat.

But Lola was no child. He almost wished she were. Then things would be easy. They'd be friends. There'd be no disturbing sizzle of sexual awareness. No hunger biting at his belly and undermining him.

Niall hadn't built a multibillion-dollar business through hard work alone. He was the public face of his company. He mixed with people all the time, he socialised, encouraged, persuaded and negotiated.

Yet with Lola he could never find the right words. His brain and his tongue disconnected. If he ran his business as badly as he'd managed his relationship with Lola he'd be bankrupt in a week.

Because beneath every interaction was that inconvenient hunger. The urgent need to do more than protect her. To ignore what he owed her family, and all the reasons he was the worst possible man for her. To bed her.

He pinched the bridge of his nose.

Bed? He'd take her on the front seat of his sports car given half a chance!

'Niall. It *is* you! I thought you weren't going to be in Queensland this week?'

He looked up into the inquisitive eyes of Carolyn Meier, doyenne of the Gold Coast social scene and formidable organiser. Quickly he surveyed the boutique, making sure Lola was still there and safe.

'Carolyn.' He got up and kissed her cheek. 'Good to see you. And you were right, I thought I'd be away.'

'But things changed?' She clapped her hands. 'Excellent. That means you can attend my party tomorrow after all. Now, don't say you can't. I need all the bidders I can get for our charity auction.'

Niall was about to shake his head when, past Carolyn's shoulder, he saw Lola through the shop window holding a negligee that consisted of a few wispy panels of lace.

Niall gulped, his throat parched. He turned to Carolyn. 'I'd love to come. If I can bring a friend.'

Because he sorely needed distraction. Attending the sort of society function he usually avoided was preferable to fighting a losing battle against his libido and Lola Suarez.

CHAPTER SEVEN

LOLA ENJOYED HERSELF ENORMOUSLY.

Despite Niall's presence.

No, she admitted, *because* of Niall.

Her words must have had some effect because he stopped hovering so obviously like the bodyguard he'd appointed himself, though he was always near enough to protect her. Which, she admitted wryly, was reassuring, despite her earlier protests.

When he relaxed and stopped trying to manage her life he was good company. So much that her hurt at his rejection eased to manageable proportions.

After all, she'd spent years berating herself over her one-sided weakness for him.

Her lips twitched as she remembered the frozen look on his face as she'd sauntered into a lingerie shop. As if it had never occurred to him that Ed's little sister was woman enough to wear such things.

Who'd have guessed the mighty, powerful Niall Pedersen would be cowed by a little silk and lace?

She'd been pleased with her tactic, she'd splurged

on some sexy underwear, simply because it appealed and she needed a boost.

She'd almost laughed at Niall's taut expression as she'd emerged from the shop carrying a petite black bag embossed with gold and tied with a gold ribbon. She'd felt feminine and carefree and she liked it.

Lola also liked the lunch place he chose. Magnificent views of the endless ocean and the best seafood she'd ever eaten. The ambience of refined opulence and the attitude of the staff, discreetly eager to please, reminded her yet again that the Niall she'd known now inhabited a completely different world from her. One of wealth and privilege.

She had another reminder when he told her they'd been invited to a party the next night. A society party, likely to be flamboyant and definitely requiring something other than the summer clothes Niall had packed for her.

Lola didn't go to lots of parties and definitely not glittering society events. Her life was humdrum as she worked hard and saved her money. She regularly told herself her turn for adventure would come when she was financially secure. But here, now, was a little adventure and she intended to enjoy it to the full.

The low point of the day came when Niall insisted he buy her a new dress for the party. If it had been anyone but Niall, the man she'd been in thrall to for years, she might have accepted. But pernickety pride got in the way.

In the end she accepted his card, had a fantastic

time trailing from one exclusive shop to another and finally bought a fantastic dress at a discounted bargain price using her own money, before returning Niall's card unused. Let him find out she hadn't spent his funds when he got his card statement.

Then, to top off the day, they'd visited an iconic wildlife park. A place she'd heard about since she was a child. They'd watched huge flocks of lorikeets swoop in to feed. Unafraid of the crowd, the birds settled everywhere, including on her arms, as they sipped the sweet nectar provided for them. Their vivid colours were a feast for the eyes and once more the difference from her own world, and the dreary end of winter in Melbourne, was stark.

Dreamily, Lola looked out across the deck of Niall's stunning retreat towards the high rises on the coast, glittering in the late afternoon light. She was in the infinity pool, her arms resting on the edge, and it felt as if she were in some fantasy world, far from mundane reality. The warmth, the scents and sounds of the forest, her buoyancy in the water, all produced a mesmerising effect that made her wish she could stay here for ever.

Not just to avoid Braithwaite, but because she hadn't felt this relaxed in ages.

Their day out yesterday had been fun in so many ways, marred only by disappointment that as soon as they returned Niall, after checking the premises' security systems, had excused himself for a conference call that must have lasted hours. She'd made herself a salad for dinner and ate alone before whiling away a few hours watching a film she'd missed at the movies.

Today, her second day in Queensland, Niall had taken her out again, this time exploring the spectacular rainforest on the edge of his mountain. But they weren't gone long, and as soon as they returned he'd headed to his office after warning her again about not answering the door. Every so often she heard him talking, presumably on business calls.

It was a reminder that, but for her, he'd be back in Brisbane, no doubt with PAs and executives in attendance, even on a Sunday.

'Have you got sunscreen on? With that pale skin you'll burn easily.'

His deep voice trawled across her bare shoulders and wound down, deep inside to the secret place that still had a weakness for Niall Pedersen.

Lola ignored that shivery feeling and rolled her eyes, telling herself he was back into big brother mode.

'I'm twenty-four, Niall, not four.'

She turned and raised her hand to shade her eyes against the afternoon sun. She could make out his tall figure on the deck but not his expression. No doubt it was concerned or disapproving. Because, despite the camaraderie they'd shared yesterday and briefly today on their bushwalk, Niall seemed borderline grumpy today.

Maybe he regretted the need to stay here with

her. It would be easier to do business at his firm's headquarters. Or maybe he'd had a date lined up for the weekend and had to cancel to babysit her.

Lola's breath snagged and her feeling of well-being dimmed. Was there some fascinating woman waiting for him in Brisbane? Was that why he sounded terse?

She plastered on a smile and spread her arms wide on the edge of the pool behind her, leisurely kicking out and enjoying the caress of warm water on bare flesh.

That had been another impulse buy yesterday. A bright red bikini, as different as possible from the modest navy one-piece in her suitcase. The thought of Niall handling that serviceable but dull swimsuit, and the memory of how he'd regretted that amazing kiss, had galvanised her into recklessness. He might see her in a bikini and think of sun protection, but *she* felt feminine in it. She lifted her chin higher.

'Coming in, Niall? It's a lovely temperature.' He'd been closeted in his office for hours. But she didn't mention that. It would sound as if she'd been keeping tabs on him.

'No. Not today.' He sounded brusque, his tension reaching her from the other side of the pool.

'Niall? What's happened? Have you heard from the police?'

She swam across the pool so she could see him properly.

'No. There's no news from Melbourne.'

But something bothered him. Lola read it in his clamped-down features. 'Bad day at the office?'

His mouth tucked up at the corner and instantly heat drilled down right through her core. She wished he wouldn't do that. Melt her insides with the merest hint of a smile.

'Something like that. I came to tell you we'll leave in an hour for this party.'

'I'll get out then.' It wouldn't take long to get ready but she'd promised herself a soak in her huge tub. The bath oil smelled heavenly and she wanted to try it.

Niall should have moved back. He hadn't expected her to pull herself straight out of the pool at his feet. But instead of swimming to the steps, she vaulted out, rising in one supple movement before him.

He should definitely have moved back *then*.

Except she stood there, all sweet, streamlined curves, gleaming wet and so desirable his mouth dried.

Surely that bikini wasn't legal?

Says the man whose lovers swim topless or naked.

But this was different. This was Lola.

It wasn't her status as Ed's sibling that made the difference. It was that he was within a hair's breadth of cupping those pert breasts with their pebbled nipples in his eager palms. Or sliding his thumbs under the side strings of her bikini and dragging the bright red fabric down her legs.

Red for passion.

For danger.

Niall's groin tightened with a heavy rush of blood. He hefted a mighty breath but couldn't fill his lungs. He tried again and only managed to take in the scent of her, wet woman and something tangy like ripe fruit.

'Excuse me.'

Lola moved, reaching for him, and hectic heat hammered in his blood.

He waited for her touch but it didn't come. Because she grabbed the towel slung over the chair beside him. The movement brought her so close he swore he felt a current of air brush him at the movement.

Finally he shuffled a step back, giving her space while she dried her shoulder-length hair.

This was why he'd kept to his study last night and today. Rousting staff from their rest in order to discuss the Asian expansion and the difficulty getting enough top-quality staff for the VIP protection teams.

To distract himself from thoughts of Lola.

Much good it had done. Whenever he looked out from his study to check on her by the pool he'd lost his train of thought. And when he didn't immediately see her he'd gone prowling, silently seeking her out to check she was safe.

How many times last night had he stood in the doorway of her bedroom, checking on her?

Of course, in his sinful thoughts, he did far more than check on her.

'You're looking forward to tonight?' His voice grated.

'I am.' Her smile lit her face, banishing the slight shadows of worry and tiredness as she wrapped the towel around her, tucking in one corner at her breast. 'I've never been to a glitzy society party. It *will* be glitzy, won't it?'

Her enthusiasm eased his tension a little. At least she had no idea of his battle with his baser self.

'It sure will.' The sort of thing he usually avoided. 'Carolyn loves to put on a show and the more publicity, the more money to her charities. There'll even be a red carpet.' Seeing Lola's eyes light up, he hurried on. 'But we won't use it. We'll take the lift from the basement.' Photographers weren't allowed at the event itself so Lola should be safe from public attention.

'Of course.' Her smile dimmed and something crushed inside him. 'Because we don't want Braithwaite finding out where I am.'

Niall nodded. He'd take no chance of Lola being snapped by paparazzi and her photo widely published, even if it seemed unlikely Braithwaite could reach her here. 'Don't worry, Lola. There'll be enough glitz to satisfy you even without the red carpet.' He paused. 'Frankly, I didn't think that would be your thing.'

She tilted her head to one side in that way she'd

always had, as if considering his words closely, and trying to read his expression.

He sure as hell hoped she couldn't tell what was going on in his mind.

'It's not. But it's been ages since I've done anything more exciting than Friday drinks after work or catching a meal and a movie with friends. I've been studying and working full-time so all my leave is used for that.' She hitched her towel higher and Niall fought not to stare at the plump, creamy skin of her breast before she covered it again. 'You know what they say, about all work and no play.'

'So you want to play tonight?' The words spilled before he could stop them. Then it was too late because all he could think of was the games he'd like to play with Lola. In private.

His body responded with predictable enthusiasm.

'A little.' Her cheerful expression slipped and he realised, belatedly, that she'd had to work at it.

A rush of sympathy hit him. Of course she had to work at it. She had a dangerous maniac out to get her. She was making the best of a bad situation, looking for distractions, and who could blame her?

Niall conjured a smile and stepped aside, gesturing for her to precede him into the house. 'Shall we? I have a feeling it's going to be a memorable night.'

Tonight would be all about Lola, not just her safety, but giving her some much-needed fun. Carolyn's party would be perfect for that.

Nothing, he assured himself, could be simpler.

CHAPTER EIGHT

LOLA ZIPPED UP the dark red dress but delayed looking in the mirror. She'd loved it in the boutique. But could she carry it off? The vivid colour, the sexy cut?

It was so not her. She dressed conservatively, partly because it suited the image she wanted to project at work. Partly because it suited her looks.

Lola was ordinary. Medium. Average.

She had dark brown hair but not as dark and lustrous as her mother's. Nor did she have her mother's flashing ebony eyes or stunning hourglass figure. Lola's eyes were an indeterminate shade of browny-green. Or was it greeny-brown? As for curves… She smoothed her palms over her hips. She had curves, just not spectacular ones.

Everyone hearing her name before meeting her expected Lola to be a stunning Latina bombshell. They were always disappointed.

Just once she'd like to live up to the promise of her exotic name.

Lola shook her head, her mouth compressing.

Since when did she think like this? Not since her teens, surely. She had a healthy, fit body and that was a blessing.

Niall. He was the reason.

Not that he'd ever given her cause to be uncomfortable about her body. He'd never commented on it.

But she'd seen photos of the glamazons he dated. Curvy, blonde and beautiful.

Just once, she'd like him to see her not as little Lola who was like a sibling to him, but as a seductive woman. She'd imagined she'd succeeded yesterday when he kissed her, until he pushed her away so fast she almost got whiplash.

She frowned, remembering his stare just now as she'd got out of the pool in front of him. He'd looked so stern it was hard to read his thoughts. She'd told herself she'd bought the bikini for herself, for the fun of it, but part of her had wondered if Niall might see her in it and…

What? Suddenly decide she was his sort of woman?

Lola snorted and reached for the stiletto sandals she'd bought with the dress. Slowly she looped the narrow leather straps once, twice around her ankle then tied them in a bow before doing up the other shoe.

One good thing about the nightmare her life had become. It had brought Niall back into her world, giving her the chance to put him behind her.

What had begun as a schoolgirl crush had turned

into something problematic. Because in a severe case of arrested development she hadn't grown out of it. Partly, she realised, because her mother's death had made her cling harder than ever to what she knew and what felt safe.

No one had made her feel safer than Niall. Well, her father had, until he turned into a stranger, going into a tailspin when he lost his wife. Everything Lola knew had wobbled on its foundations.

Then, while Lola had become more and more cautious, her friends had started dating. She, as the sensible one, the good listener, had been the recipient of so many confidences about sexual experiences gone wrong, dating disasters, predatory and dangerously aggressive boyfriends, it had fed her natural caution in ever-diminishing circles.

Till she'd been almost afraid to date.

By the time she did, she was primed to expect disaster. All the time, at the back of her mind, was the mirage of Niall Pedersen. Not the real man but the fantasy she'd built him into in her head. She'd extrapolated on his kindness and his phenomenal looks and turned him into an ideal man against whom no one could compete.

Was it any wonder her love life was non-existent?

The time had come to do something about it.

When she'd bought this outfit she'd wondered if it would alter Niall's view of her. He wasn't as immune to her as he pretended. Inner muscles clenched as she remembered being clamped against his erection when they'd kissed.

Maybe, wonder of wonders, she'd end this ridiculous crush with a night in his bed. From what her friends said, he wouldn't seem nearly so amazing after that. And it would be a chance to burn off the sexual frustration that had reached dangerous heights.

Lola shook her head. She was determined not to think about Niall. They had no future. He'd made that clear. Instead she'd enjoy her glamorous party and test out her underdeveloped flirting skills on a stranger or two.

She'd turn over a new leaf. When she got home, and when she got free of Braithwaite, she'd start dating seriously. She'd relegate Niall to the past and get on with life.

Swinging around, she surveyed herself in the mirror.

She looked…different.

Lola hadn't straightened her hair or put it up. She told herself the unbound waves suited the look.

The dress clasped her body close down to her hips before flaring a little around her thighs. She wore no bra since the dress was cut so low at the back but she liked the narrow double straps, just wide enough for a row of diamantés, that rose over each shoulder and crossed on her back. And the shoes… Lola smiled at the spiky, sexy heels.

She didn't look like ordinary Lola Suarez any more.

Lifting her chin, she met her eyes in the mirror. It didn't matter that she wasn't Niall's type. She was her own woman and intended to enjoy herself.

'I'm ready.'

Niall swung round and Lola repressed a shiver of nervous excitement.

So he looked a million dollars. So what? He wasn't for her. Nor did it matter if he approved of how she looked.

Yet her gaze lingered on the blue shirt that matched his eyes, and the pale jacket and trousers that made the most of his tall, lean frame, accentuating the dark gold of his skin.

Tropical dressy and pure gorgeousness. That was how he looked.

Lola ignored her suddenly erratic pulse, telling herself it was excitement about the party. She also tamped down a wriggle of discomfort, imagining all the women who'd cluster around him tonight. Good! That would leave her free to enjoy herself. She didn't need a babysitter.

'You look…' He stopped speaking as she moved from the dim hallway into the light.

She saw the hint of a frown pinch his forehead and all at once he looked stern, the angles and planes of his face hard and angular.

'Glamorous?' she prompted, jutting one hip and

posing with her hand at her waist as if she hadn't a care in the world. 'Just right for a glitzy party?' She spun on the spot, her skirt twirling around her bare legs.

'Very nice.'

Nice! Lola's mouth tightened. Even Ed could do better than that and he rarely noticed anything without feathers or fur.

For a second she wondered if she'd made a mistake, buying this dress. But only for a second. She liked how she looked. She didn't need Niall's approval.

'Have you got a cardigan? You might get cold.'

Lola blinked. It was like hearing a voice from the past. In her teens, her father had expected her to carry a cardigan in case it got cold, an umbrella in case it rained and a tissue. Beside him, her mother would just smile and tell her to enjoy herself. After her mother died, Lola's outings were curtailed and for a long time her father hadn't noticed her, much less what she wore.

'I'm sure I'll be fine.' She moved towards the door. 'Shall we go?'

For a long moment Niall said nothing. She even wondered if he'd changed his mind. Then, abruptly, he stalked towards her.

Despite her determination not to be affected, her heart fluttered as he approached, his stride all fluid power. Then she turned and preceded him through the door.

The drive down the mountain was different. Niall drove with the same ease and focus but something new simmered in the air between them.

'Are you having trouble at work?' she asked eventually.

'What makes you think so?'

'Surely even a self-made billionaire has Sundays off.'

He shrugged. 'A few issues needed personal attention.'

Lola shifted in her seat, hating the way her wayward imagination linked the shiver-deep voice with the words *personal attention*.

With luck she'd spend the evening chatting up some gorgeous, fascinating guy. Someone who didn't remind her of Niall. Though if he had a rich, deep voice it wouldn't hurt. And a hard, powerful body.

She shifted again. The upholstery was even softer than she remembered, possibly because her dress was so short she felt the leather against bare skin.

It was a relief when they reached the city and, as they skirted a block where a crowd had gathered on the pavement, Lola was glad they weren't making a red-carpet entrance. She intended to enjoy herself but wasn't sure she had the confidence for that.

As Niall ushered her into the lift from the basement carpark, he finally spoke, breaking her thoughts.

'You look more than nice.' His words yanked

her face up towards his. A shot of blue fire blasted through her. 'You look fabulous.'

Lola waited for that indefinable something in his expression that told her he exaggerated, probably to boost her confidence after his earlier, lukewarm response. It didn't come.

Instead there was just his bright stare and a steady burn of admiration that warmed her from the inside out.

Her breath snagged behind her ribs and her lungs felt too tight. She drew in a quick breath, hyper-aware of the sharp rise of her braless breasts against thin silk.

'Thank you. So do you.' She licked her lips, her mouth suddenly dry.

Niall's gaze dropped to her lips and something shifted inside. That heat settled low in her abdomen and—

The lift doors opened and they were no longer alone.

They stepped straight into an amazing apartment, and into the heart of a flamboyant celebration.

The place was packed. There were people and movement everywhere and the lavishly decorated setting made Lola's eyes widen as Niall led her forward.

A huge atrium extended up over three floors with a curving marble staircase and a vast, shallow pool at its base. The enormous space was decked out like an exuberantly decorated circus tent. But more lavish than a real tent. There were swathes of silks, satins and bling everywhere.

Wait staff wended their way through the throng on unicycles, balancing trays of bubbly and incredible cocktails adorned with fruit and fizzing sparklers. Tightrope walkers danced overhead and acrobats, dressed in lavish outfits that seemed to consist mainly of sparkling crystal, performed amazing feats. There was even a fire-eater, ankle-deep in the sapphire-tiled pool.

'He's probably in the water as a safety precaution,' Niall bent close to murmur, his breath warm on her ear. 'Last year Carolyn insisted on lighting Catherine wheels inside and there was a slight problem. She doesn't do things by halves.'

'It's amazing.' Lola breathed, trying not to notice the way her cheek tingled from the caress of his breath. Instead she focused on the throng of guests, some in casual clothes and others dressed to the nines in stunning displays of wearable wealth. 'It's...'

'Gaudy? Over the top?' She turned to find a blonde woman beside her, her trim form spectacular in a beautifully tailored ringmaster's outfit. Instead of a bow tie, she sported the most amazing necklace Lola had ever seen. If they were real diamonds... 'I hope so, darling. I wanted something people wouldn't forget in a hurry. Though I did have my heart set on having an elephant too. But Ted, my husband, made such a fuss about trying to get even

a baby elephant into the lift, and then I remembered
we don't support animals in circuses any more, so
maybe it wasn't such a good idea.'

The woman grinned, her gap-toothed smile so
warm Lola forgot the fortune in gems she wore.
'I'm Carolyn. You must be Niall's friend.'

'Lola.' She smiled back. 'Thank you so much for
inviting me.' Automatically she put out her hand as
she did at work, then wondered if rich people air-
kissed instead.

But Carolyn's handshake was firm and friendly.
'I'm pleased to meet you.' She darted a look at Niall
that Lola couldn't read. 'Absolutely delighted. Anything you want, just ask. Meanwhile, let me intro-
duce you...'

They were swept up into a round of introductions
that made Lola's head spin. The guests included a
raft of VIPs she knew by repute. International movie
stars and directors, on the coast for filming. Famous
authors and artists. Billionaires and philanthropists.
A naturalist documentary maker whose face was
famous the world over. He knew Ed's work and mo-
nopolised her until Niall interrupted, saying there
was someone she needed to meet.

That someone was Jake, an advertising execu-
tive, way above Lola's paygrade, but personable and
pleasant, and happy to talk about building a career
in the industry.

Niall moved away and Lola was glad he didn't

hover. Though time and again she'd look up from a conversation to find his dark eyes on her.

Was he in bodyguard mode? Or making sure she didn't feel out of her depth? He needn't worry. She was having a great time.

Lola turned back to Jake, who asked her about her career plans. He really was very nice. Handsome too, with his surfer blond good looks, and thoughtful, snagging her a fresh glass of wine from a passing waiter.

She just wished she couldn't still feel Niall's eyes on her. Or the betraying kernel of tension deep inside that had nothing to do with the party or Braithwaite and everything to do with the crush she was determined to end sooner rather than later.

So when Jake asked her if she wanted to dance, she gulped down a mouthful of crisp white wine and put her glass aside, smiling her assent. 'I'd love to. Thank you.'

Niall had made plenty of mistakes in his time but none as significant as this one.

He should never have brought her here.
Never have introduced her to Jake Sinclair.

Bad enough to watch Jake dance with Lola earlier, when the music was loud and upbeat. But now, hours later, the music had changed and the dancers moved slowly, in what looked more like slowly savoured sex than dancing.

Pain shot up Niall's jaw and he realised he was grinding his molars. Again.

Breaking away from the knot of people around him, ignoring the clutch of feminine fingers on his arm and the invitation in a pair of bright blue eyes, Niall shouldered his way through the throng to a relatively quiet spot where he could watch the dance floor and brood in peace.

Except there'd be no peace, not with Lola, gorgeous in that red dress and come-take-me heels that emphasised the slender shape of her legs and drew the eye up to her ripe peach of a derriere. Not when she was plastered against a grinning Jake Sinclair.

Multiple times tonight Niall had intervened, steering Lola towards new acquaintances he thought she'd enjoy. Staying beside her during the fundraising auction and enjoying her enthusiasm when he'd won various items. He'd found any excuse to remove her from Jake and that appreciative glint in his eye. But whenever he left her Jake turned up again.

Yet Niall had been compelled to give her space. Lola hated being reminded of the reasons for his protectiveness and he'd vowed tonight would be about her enjoying herself after the stress of recent days. More importantly, if he stayed beside her he might give in to the desperate urge to touch her himself.

His belly clenched as he watched her move sinuously, every slim line and curve revealed by the tight, short dress that had lit a hungry flame inside him.

Back at the house he'd been on the verge of telling her the party had been cancelled and they had to stay in. Except that would mean an evening alone in her company. An evening with a temptress dressed to party…and seduce.

Niall was strong-willed. Apart from that one kiss, he'd stood firm against his baser instincts from the moment he'd walked into Lola's apartment a few days ago. But there were limits and he'd reached his.

The voice of his conscience, reminding him that he owed her a duty of care—that he couldn't, shouldn't, mustn't touch her—had been silent since she sashayed out of her bedroom looking like a sexy angel from a wet dream.

He hefted in a draught of air that did nothing to cool the deep-seated pulse of need throbbing through him.

Niall knew what Jake Sinclair wanted. Because he wanted the same. Lola, naked in his bed. Or, his temperature spiked, still in that dress, as she rode his erection while he held her hips and feasted on her tantalising breasts through the red fabric. Niall swallowed hard and gulped down the whisky he'd moved on to when beer failed to slake his thirst.

Nothing would slake his thirst but Lola.

His only consolation was that Jake wouldn't get her either. Not on Niall's watch.

Lola was safe tonight from Braithwaite, given

the tighter security arrangements he'd arranged for the building. Even so Niall was on constant alert for any hint of danger.

He'd also make sure she was safe from casual philanderers. This was the first time she'd danced with Jake in thirty minutes. It would be the last. But he'd wait till the music stopped before intervening. He had that much control, just.

Jake's hand slid down her hip, drawing her closer, and a growl built at the back of Niall's throat.

'If you don't like it, do something about it, darling.'

He turned to find Carolyn at his elbow, looking at Lola and Jake.

'I will. Soon.' When this never-ending song finished. 'She deserves a chance to enjoy herself.'

'At your expense?' Carolyn slanted him a curious look. 'From what I saw she'd be happier dancing with you.'

Niall turned back towards the dancers. 'She looks happy to me.' His voice hit a rough note and he swallowed a little more whisky, easing his dry throat.

'Ah, but you haven't seen the way she's been looking at you all night. Funny that you haven't noticed. But then you've gone to such trouble not to stare at her all the time. Till now.'

Could it be true? Would Lola prefer to be with him?

Niall reminded himself it wasn't possible. It wouldn't be right.

But his body had other ideas. The music ended and he strode forward, thrusting his glass into Carolyn's hand, the sound of her chuckle in his ears.

He wasn't in the habit of revealing weakness. But right now he didn't care that his hostess had read him like a book. All he cared for was…

'My dance.' No please. No hesitation. Just his hand on Jake's shoulder, pulling him away, and his other hand on Lola's. Her eyes met his and the fire in his belly dropped straight to his groin.

Carolyn had been right. He saw excitement flare in Lola's eyes, her lips parting as if she drew in a sudden breath.

Jake said something Niall didn't hear as he pulled Lola towards him and, miracle of miracles, she settled against him, her slender body fitting close.

Niall sucked in a shaky breath as his brain struggled to catalogue all the many ways this felt good. Finally he gave up and simply basked in the rush of pleasure. After a moment he noticed the music and remembered to move. It was no more than a shuffle, but it brought Lola against him in new and delicious ways.

Was that a sigh? He gathered her nearer, tilting her head against his shoulder and bending his head to inhale the summer sunshine scent of her hair.

Another wash of desire filled him and he slipped his hand to her hip, wondering if she'd object. Instead she moved closer and his thigh insinuated between her legs as they turned.

Niall's hand slid further, lower, till he claimed her buttock and then a new heat blasted him. The heat of her sex rubbing against him.

Need jolted through him so hard he forgot they were supposed to be dancing. He stood, rock hard, his leg pressing between hers, his hand drawing her to him in a movement that was purely, overtly sexual.

He had to stop this. Had to remember why he couldn't—

'Niall? Don't you want to dance any more?'

She looked up and he was drowning in soft green. It was like looking into the rainforest, greens and darker flecks of shadow beckoning him closer.

He opened his mouth then shut it again. He didn't trust himself to speak. If he vocalised he feared it might be an utterly feral roar of possessiveness.

Then he saw her mouth turn down at the corners and some of the light dim in her lovely eyes.

'No,' he said at last, his voice thick. 'It's not dancing I want.'

Her lips, the lips that had been so soft against his, formed into an O of surprise.

Not rejection or distaste.

She lifted her hand from his shoulder and raked her fingers through the hair on the back of his head. Instinctively he tipped his head back into her touch as tingling ripples of pleasure cascaded from her fingertips.

If it felt that good when she merely touched his scalp…

'Nor me,' she murmured in a throaty voice that untied another row of knots in the web of his self-control.

Niall frowned, trying to make sense of her words. Then she moved against him in a suggestive sway that blasted everything else into the background.

'Hold that thought,' he growled. Drawing together the tattered fibres of his self-possession, he stepped back, ignoring his body's silent scream of protest. He was strung so tight it was a wonder he could even make the move.

The only positive was seeing his own distress mirrored in Lola's eyes.

He threaded his fingers through hers and led her to the edge of the room. He felt clumsy, his gait stiff-legged because of the hard-on he could do nothing about.

Not yet. But soon. Meanwhile his body felt as if it were stretched on a rack, taut to the edge of pain.

Faces blurred as they passed. People spoke but he didn't stop. Then, near the lift, he spied a familiar blonde, her top hat tipped at a jaunty angle, a cocktail in one hand and her finger on the button for the lift.

'Darlings! I'm so pleased you had a good time.' Niall read a mischievous twinkle in Carolyn's eyes.

'I had a feeling you might be leaving. Ah, here it is.'
She turned and, with a flourish, gestured for them
to step inside.

'Thanks, Carolyn. It's been…memorable.'

Lola added her thanks before the doors shut, en-
closing them together. Instantly his tension ratcheted
from extreme to the catastrophic. His pulse thundered and her perfume in his nostrils threatened to
short-circuit his senses.

Niall punched in his private access code with
an unsteady hand, then leaned forward for the iris
scanner he'd insisted on during the building phase.

He kept his attention on the display panel because he feared if he looked at Lola the security
staff monitoring the cameras would get an eyeful
of their boss having unbridled sex with the temptress beside him.

But he kept tight hold of her hand.

Niall swallowed hard. When had holding hands
become an erotic experience?

Touching Lola's soft palm, her slim fingers
threaded through his, felt like a promise of what was
to come. Soon he'd feel her smooth body against
him as they melded together completely.

He swallowed again, his skin steaming despite
the perfectly stable temperature.

'We're going up, not down.'

He had to concentrate on making his voice work.
'I had more to drink than I intended.' Because the
sight of Lola cosying up to Jake Sinclair drove him

to ignore his usual limits. 'I won't take a chance on being over the limit. We'll stay here the night.'

'You have an apartment here as well as on the mountain?'

Ridiculous how tough it was to concentrate on conversation.

'An investment.' The whole building was, but he kept the penthouse for himself. He'd rent it out now he had the house in the hinterland. The doors opened and they stepped into the penthouse.

A swish of sound as the doors closed, leaving them cut off from the outside world. The air rushed from Niall's lungs and some of the corded tension in his tortured muscles eased.

At last.

He turned to the woman beside him. The woman who drove him to the edge of reason. Sure enough, one glance at those wide eyes and parted lips, and something slammed down inside him.

The voice of caution smashing into oblivion?

Because nothing, not conscience or good intentions or even guilt, could make him release her now.

He'd gone past the point of no return. Unless…

'Lola.' His tongue was thick and his voice husky. 'If you don't want me, say so now. Then choose a bedroom and shut the door and you won't see me till tomorrow.'

How he'd find the strength to deliver on the promise he didn't know. But one thing at a time.

She shook her head and his hand tightened, dismay filling him. Had he misread——?

Lola's gaze locked on his. The impact was a pulse of energy straight to his groin. 'I want you, Niall. So much.'

CHAPTER NINE

HE TOOK HER mouth so fast he tasted his name on her lips.

No, that was the taste of Lola. Once experienced, impossible to forget.

The sweet tang had haunted him.

How often had he woken from fitful sleep to the memory of her flavour on his tongue? Hungering for the full banquet of her luscious body instead of a mere taste?

He hauled her close, softness against hard, needy flesh, and felt the vibrations as his last reserves of caution crashed down. Her lips were soft, her mouth accommodating yet demanding, everything he remembered and so much more.

A shudder shot from his nape, down between his shoulder blades to the soles of his feet. Her smoky, seductive voice still echoed in his ears.

She wanted him.

The way she slid up against him, as if trying to meld herself to his erection, was better than any fantasy. Stars exploded at the corners of his vision but putting any distance between them was impossible.

One hand cradling her skull, Niall leaned into the kiss, bending her backwards so she clung. His might be the dominant position but there was nothing submissive about Lola. She devoured him with a hungry fervour that catapulted his need higher. And that low humming sound in the back of her throat—part approval, part demand—ignited his blood like a flame touching oil.

The kiss deepened, became a mating of mouths, mirroring the sex act they both needed so desperately.

Niall couldn't remember a kiss ever being like this—the most erotic foreplay. And the most devastating.

His chest cramped as he lost oxygen and forgot to breathe in more.

Frantic to touch, he dropped his hand from Lola's waist to mould her buttock, pulling her in even harder. She circled her pelvis against him and he froze, clawing at the ragged remnants of his restraint.

'Wait,' he groaned. 'Stop.'

Clamping her with both hands now, he held her still. One more undulation and she'd undo him. Heart hammering, he eased away just enough to suck in air.

'But I want—'

Another time he might have triumphed at the

sulky pout in her voice, and on her kiss-swollen mouth. Now all he could do was pray he didn't embarrass himself.

'I know, sweetheart. Me too. But give me a moment.'

Another first. He'd never teetered on the edge of climax after just a kiss, and fully clothed at that.

He pressed a kiss to her neck, to that fragrant curve, and felt her shiver as she tilted her head to give him better access.

Niall slid his hands possessively and frowned. He felt only taut curves and slippery silk but no underwear.

Snapping open eyes he hadn't realised he'd closed, he looked beyond her to the full-length mirror on the opposite wall of the entry. Saw his hands on the shimmery red dress, hauling it higher and higher until it was no longer silk he touched but even softer flesh. Bare, pale flesh bisected by the tiniest line of dark red lace.

G-strings were nothing new. Once a lover had come to him wearing nothing but a raincoat and crotchless knickers. But that memory was blurred. Nothing, ever, had looked as sexy as Lola's pert bottom with that suggestive sliver of lace.

There was a galloping sound in his ears and a rushing pressure driving down between his legs. Niall was on the verge of spilling himself like an over-excited schoolkid.

'Wait,' he said again, nipping the curve where her neck met her shoulder and feeling her tremble.

Before she could object, Niall stepped back, putting a whole centimetre of space between them, even though the savage beast inside him howled a protest.

Dreamy green eyes opened, catching his gaze, but refusing to be snared, and ruthless with the need to make this last, Niall moved her up against the wall.

Then he dropped to his knees.

In her high heels she was just at the right height.

Anticipation sizzled as he yanked her teasing little skirt up at the front. Past slim thighs that trembled, till he found the V of scarlet lace.

He exhaled on a rush of pleasure. Then saw her twitch as his breath warmed her skin. Her hand appeared, making to cover the treasure he'd found.

But she didn't resist when he took her hand and pulled it away. One palm still pinning her skirt against her belly, he raised her hand to his mouth as he lifted his gaze.

Her mouth was open on a sigh of pleasure. When he licked across her palm and up the length of her index finger she swallowed convulsively, her wide eyes narrowing under weighted lids.

He'd barely started and the mere sight of her undid him.

She looked sultry and inviting, yet something

about her made him think of some goddess, alluring but untouchable.

Except he *was* touching her. He intended to brand himself on her body so thoroughly that she couldn't think straight.

Taking his time, he laved the next finger and the next, drawing each into his mouth and sucking.

A small, keening sound reached his ears and he felt her tremble.

'Niall.'

The way she said his name was like a prayer and a demand, urgent and reverent at the same time, making him feel like some sort of conquering hero. He wanted to hear Lola say his name like that again and again. He wanted to hear her scream it as she came, convulsing around him.

His erection throbbed against the confines of his clothes but he did his best to ignore that, focusing on Lola.

Releasing her hand, he leaned forward, pressing his mouth against red lace that was already gratifyingly damp, drawing slowly against that intimate heat till she shook even harder. Her scent was more concentrated here, sweet and tart with a hint of womanly musk.

Niall's hands were unsteady as he peeled the tiny strips of lace from her hips, rolling them down her legs. She tried to step out but the lace caught first on the sexy leather bow at her ankle, then on her spike heel.

He heard a muffled sob and offered soothing words as he helped her free.

Then his fragile patience ended. Pushing her thighs apart, he leaned forward, breathing in her rich perfume and sinking his face against dark, downy curls.

Lola clutched him, one hand to his shoulder, the other in his hair.

One exploratory flick of his tongue and she cried out, greedily bucking her hips. He smiled, licking again, slower and further, and felt her shudder.

Lola's breathing fractured and he felt her thigh muscles tense. He barely had time to delve with first one finger, then a second, when she screamed. Her frantic convulsions squeezed his fingers as her thighs pushed against him.

Remarkably, Niall almost came with her. He was so ready that feeling and tasting Lola's climax, the first he'd given her, almost sent him over the edge.

Fingernails scraped his scalp and he welcomed the sting, giving him something to concentrate on other than the urge to lose himself.

Lola wilted and he uncoiled, rising and lifting her into his arms in the same movement.

She was limp and delectable.

Nudging her hair aside, he slid his lips across her cheek to her mouth and was rewarded with instant entry. This time their kiss held a new element. A languorous welcome from the woman he'd pleasured to screaming point. Did she taste herself on his lips?

Niall had to move. Despite the fact that walking was near impossible because his body was so primed. Because he wanted Lola horizontal and naked.

Somehow, mouth still fused with hers, he navigated past the reception rooms to the bedrooms, guided by the low lighting that had switched on when they entered.

He veered into the first bedroom, stopping before the bed to put her on her feet. He needed to be out of his trousers and wearing protection before he lay against her.

One easy glide and her zip was down, but those crossed shoulder straps...

'Let me.' Lola's voice was a throaty purr and he actually took a half-step back as he peeled off his jacket and ripped at his shirt. Because any more incitement would be too much.

His wallet was in his hand, fingers freeing a condom, when Lola's beautiful dress slid to the floor.

All the air left Niall's lungs in a rush of appreciation.

'You're gorgeous.'

He'd known it from the first. The moment in Melbourne when she'd opened her door to him he'd seen she'd grown into her early promise. But knowing and seeing every bare inch—they were two different things.

His gaze skated down then lingered, slow on the way back up. Her fingers twitched, hands moving as if to cover herself. Then her chin lifted and her hands dropped to her sides.

Wasn't she used to being naked with her lovers? With her beautiful, streamlined curves, she had a body any man would desire.

'I want to touch you but I don't dare.' His voice was like hot tar spilling across gravel and the constriction in his throat tightened when Lola's lips curled at the corners.

She was bewitching. Tantalising. Effortlessly sexy and yet once more he was struck by the idea of an untouchable ideal. A woman far removed from the normal run.

'I want to touch you too.'

She made it sound like a husky invitation and Niall had to stop himself from moving closer. Instead his hands went to his belt, fumbling with the buckle and fastening as if they were unfamiliar puzzles. Toeing off his shoes, he stripped off clothes and sheathed himself. He did it with his eyes closed because the sight of Lola's direct gaze as his hands moved to his penis was temptation overload.

When he looked again it was to see her slick her tongue over her bottom lip, her attention still on his groin. On cue, his erection bobbed higher, rampantly eager.

Lola chuckled and for a moment he thought she

sounded nervous as well as amused. But she didn't look nervous. She looked *hungry*.

Niall grabbed her hand and led her to the bed, careful not to touch her anywhere else. Despite the way his eyes kept returning to those tip-tilted breasts.

'What did you say?' Her voice was barely audible.

'Nothing.' His mouth must have moved as he mentally ran through his thirteen times table, trying to focus on something other than Lola's bare body and the ecstasy that beckoned.

He didn't get past twenty-six. Because then she lay down on the bed, all lean muscle and sinuous, elegant curves. Her raspberry-crested breasts wobbled as she shuffled across to make space for him.

Niall didn't need space. He had no intention of lying anywhere but between her thighs.

He joined her, kneeling above her with his hands planted near her shoulders. It was like having a banquet set before him and not knowing where to begin. His lower body was taut and heavy with need, ready to take. But he summoned a little finesse, wanting her eager for him again.

Keeping his hands on the bed, he lowered his head to her breast, exploring the satiny, scented skin with his lips and tongue, till she was twitching beneath him, her breath coming in rough pants. Smiling, he moved to her other breast, teasing that ripe nipple with his teeth, to be rewarded with a cry of muffled desperation.

Lola's thighs fell open between his knees and her hands clamped his head to her breast, as if fearing he might leave before finishing what he'd started.

No chance of that.

Shoving her legs wider with his knees, he settled in the cradle of her hips, his smile turning to a grimace as the impact of their bodies touching blasted through him.

Desperate, he slid his hand between them, down that dainty cleft and up into moist heat. Instantly she lifted, seeking more, and his last restraint snapped.

One elbow on the bed, he guided himself to her, delaying only a second to appreciate the moment as her forest green eyes ate him up. Then, with one sure, hard thrust, he took her.

He thought he'd known. Thought he was prepared.

But nothing had readied him for Lola. So incredibly tight, so slick and—

'Niall!' It wasn't a scream of ecstasy but a whisper of shock.

He was shocked at the unexpected impediment that turned out to be no barrier at all as his momentum took him into Lola's sweet, mind-numbing heat.

He knew a momentary impulse to stop. Actually withdrawing was impossible. But by then it was over and he nestled right at her core. They fitted together so snugly he couldn't but savour it.

A shudder racked him so deeply it seemed to start in his bone marrow and work out.

Lifting a hand that trembled because of the effort it took to remain still, Niall brushed the hair off her face. He tried to read her expression. Her shock had faded and thankfully he saw no sign of pain.

Had he hurt her?

'Are you all right, sweetheart?'

Her skin was flushed and damp and her eyes veiled, as if hiding secrets.

But her biggest secret was out.

Lola had been a virgin!

Finally his thinking brain caught up with his physical instincts and guilt smote him.

Lola, a virgin.

He was rearing up when her hands clamped to his shoulders. A silky calf slid up and over his backside and everything inside him shouted hallelujah.

Niall gritted his teeth, torn between guilt and desire.

Her beautiful eyes held his and just like that his internal struggle ended.

Who did he think he was fooling? Pulling back was impossible.

He lowered his head, nuzzling her neck, down to that most sensitive spot that made her gasp and wriggle beneath him.

That was all it took, the sound of her breath, and that tiny shimmy of her hips, and he was gone.

Niall captured her lips, claiming her mouth as his body took hers, pumping smooth and fast, each slide into her untried depths producing the most phenomenal joy he'd ever known.

Seconds later he was beyond thought.

Primitive instinct, not conscious decision, made him bite gently at her neck, his fingers slipping between her legs as the firestorm exploded in his blood. He rammed his body into hers, all control lost.

Through the blurring haze, Niall felt Lola's muscles contract and caress him, as urgent and heedless as his own bucking spasms.

'Lola.' It was a silent cry of triumph against her lips as ecstasy dragged him under.

CHAPTER TEN

LOLA HEARD MOVEMENT, water running, but was still riding high on adrenaline and sexual satisfaction.

She smiled into the downy soft pillow.

Making love with Niall was beyond anything she'd imagined.

Hot and urgent, but even a novice could appreciate the effort he'd put into ensuring her pleasure.

When he'd gone down on his knees before her! Her heart rolled over at the thought and muscles deep inside, muscles she'd barely been aware of before tonight, tightened.

A shiver of voluptuous reminiscence shook her.

It had been worth the wait. She understood instinctively that sex with anyone else wouldn't have been like this.

Did Niall feel this indescribable wonder too?

It was unlikely. Surely her response was amplified because all this was new to her.

And because it was Niall. The man she'd fixated on for half her life.

Her heart felt overfull, as if the emotions she'd

bottled up so long were bursting out and bubbling over. The enormity of merging her body with his had untied something locked tight within her. Something she'd strived half her life to hide.

What they shared had seemed momentous, far more than a physical act. So profound, it was as if the earth tilted around them. Lola felt undone by the enormity of her feelings and at the same time strengthened by them.

But she knew better than to mention them to Niall. He didn't feel the same. A shadow dimmed her pleasure but she ignored it. She refused to pine for the moon tonight when Niall had taken her to the stars. She still felt the glitter of that pulsating white light deep within.

He'd been so passionate. He hadn't been taking pity on her, the poor victim of a stalker. He'd been with her every step of the way.

Tonight Lola had been excited to discover that the particularly grim expression Niall wore from time to time, when those chiselled features turned stone-like and the pulse at his jaw flicked hard, betrayed arousal.

Her lips curved at the thought of how very aroused Niall had been. Enormously aroused.

A giggle escaped, the sound loud in the quiet room.

She opened her eyes and saw the rim of light around the bathroom door.

Surely he was taking a long time to dispose of a condom?

But then, with that water running, he must be showering.

Lola rolled onto her back, minutely conscious of the cool sheet beneath her heated skin, the slide of her thighs against each other, and the wet, swollen feeling of fullness between her legs.

Yet, even sated, she felt the tiniest lick of heat in her belly as she thought of Niall, naked, with water sluicing down his strong back and over those tightly curved buttocks.

One hand had grabbed him there as he'd powered into her and it had been phenomenally exciting, feeling the bunch of taut muscle as he thrust deep inside.

The little flicker of heat grew to a flame.

How would he react if she joined him in the shower? If she caressed him the way he'd caressed her?

There was only one complication. She didn't think her legs would move. Her bones had disintegrated when he took her to the stars a second time and now her limbs were heavy. The only parts of her that still worked were her buzzing brain and that gently throbbing spot between her legs.

The door opened and Niall stood there, broad shoulders and tapering figure outlined by the light.

Lola's mouth dried. He looked so good.

She couldn't read his expression with the light

behind him and wondered if he could see hers. Did she look dreamy-eyed? She didn't care. Not when he was striding across to her and the yearning she'd never been able to suppress swamped her, stronger than ever.

This man.

Only ever *this* man.

Whatever the reason, it had only ever been Niall Pedersen for her.

But he didn't join her in bed. Instead he bent down and lifted her, his arms cradling her naked body as he straightened.

Lola registered again the exciting, teasing prickle of his chest hair against her skin. Flesh to flesh, held close in those powerful arms, was a potent reinforcement of his maleness and her femininity. Of how perfectly they matched.

This was blisteringly, fiercely real. Far beyond her previous, pallid imaginings.

She shivered and his hands tightened.

'Are you okay? Did I hurt you very much?' Niall's voice sounded curiously stretched.

'No.' Not enough to complain about and the discomfort was swiftly gone. Lola leaned into him, her palm against his neck, breathing in the fresh scent of citrus soap and damp male flesh. 'You showered.' Disappointment stirred.

She felt his breath shudder out.

Because of her? Because of her touch?

There was so much she didn't know, so much she wanted to learn about him, about them.

'I've run you a bath. It might relax you after... It might help if you're sore.'

Never in her life had Niall sounded anything but certain. Even as a rangy, spiky teenager, wary of trusting others, he'd always projected an air of self-assurance.

His thoughtfulness touched her.

But then it always had. Right from the first, she'd sensed she could trust him.

'Thanks, Niall.' She leaned her face against him, breathing him in. Wishing she could stay exactly where she was. But a moment later he was lowering her feet into water.

'How's the temperature?'

'Perfect. Thank you.' The warmth caressed her soles, making her aware of small aches and the kernel of tenderness between her legs.

Seconds later she was shoulder deep in the huge bath, her eyelids riding low as the last, lingering tension left her body. Bliss!

Movement caught her attention, made her sit up.

'You're leaving?' Usually she was good at hiding her feelings from him, but even she heard the hurt in her voice.

'I thought you'd like privacy.' Niall's features were unreadable, his eyes watchful.

What she'd like was for him to join her. To hold her in his arms while they shared the aftermath of the single most remarkable experience of her life. To prolong that profound sense of oneness.

Caution stopped her blurting all that out. If she couldn't have the fantasy, she could come close.

'Won't you keep me company? Please?'

Finally he moved, but not, as she'd hoped, into the bath with her. Her body might be limp but her mind was very, very active when it came to Niall.

He settled on a low padded chair she hadn't even noticed in the opulent, mirrored and marbled bathroom. It was at the far end of the bath and he sat facing slightly away from her. Over the rim of the high bath she could only see his head and chest, and she felt a pang of regret at the distance, the lack of physical contact.

His black eyebrows crunched down in a frown. 'How do you feel?'

'Terrific!'

His eyes widened and she almost laughed at his patent surprise.

'Well, worn out, but in the most delicious way.' She shivered, remembering how they'd been together, and felt internal muscles twitch. Water lapped around her shoulders like a caress.

Niall's gaze, almost ebony in this light, held hers as if he sifted her words. What was going on in his head?

He swallowed, his Adam's apple bobbing hard in his throat. It was all he could do to stay here, pretending he was glued to the seat, and not climb into that oversized tub and expand Lola's sexual experience a whole lot more.

His skin prickled tight despite the warm fug of steamy air.

He'd just had raw, lusty sex with Lola.

His best friend's little sister.

The woman he'd vowed to protect.

For days he'd repeated that mantra. Hoping reinforcement would prevent him acting on urges a better man would resist.

The prickle turned to a shudder as he tried and failed not to notice her glistening pink-washed skin. The bob of cherry-dark nipples cresting the surface of the water as she sat higher.

There'd been cherries on her cotton knickers in Melbourne.

He blinked, trying to divert his thoughts from ripe fruit and cherries in particular. And what he'd just done. But there was nowhere to go. Just into the swamp of self-disgust at ravaging her innocence or straight back into lust, as if he hadn't just taken his fill.

Yet now he was ready for more.

Niall swung his gaze away and found himself staring through the open door at the rumpled bed, surrounded by a spray of discarded clothes.

It had been no tender wooing. Yes, he'd ensured she climaxed. The first time with his face between her legs, jammed up against a wall barely one step inside the apartment! The second with him rutting, hard and fast, more animal than civilised man. The flesh at his nape crawled.

'I wish I'd known you were inexperienced.'

Without intending to, he turned his head, his gaze snagging on hers. His heart pounded so hard he felt it rise in his throat.

'Then you wouldn't have made love to me.'

Niall sucked in air. He'd like to believe she was right. Yet he had an unedifying suspicion even that wouldn't have stopped him. He'd been driven by a primitive force so compelling nothing short of the building falling around their ears would have got in the way.

'You're not going all quaint on me, are you, Niall? Everyone has a first time.' Her nipples crested the water again as she took a breath. 'I'm glad mine was with you.'

Then she gave him that smile. The one that sent his brains corkscrewing down to his groin. It wasn't a deliberately sexy smile, but her pleasure and her honesty undid every knot and frayed rope in the barrier he'd been trying to cobble together since leaving the bed.

The trouble was, he was glad too. Because he couldn't stomach the idea of her with any other man.

Yet inevitably guilt cast its shadow.

Her smile faded, drooping at the edges, and he realised she'd read his silence.

'I feel honoured, Lola.'

She shook her head, dark waves swishing around her shoulders. 'You *are* going old-fashioned on me. I can see it in your face.' In one sudden movement she sat up completely, baring her beautiful breasts, her hands clutching the sides of the tub. 'Don't spoil it by going all poker-faced, Niall.'

Despite himself that dragged a huff of laughter from him. 'Poker-faced? Is that what I am?'

Good thing that, where she sat she couldn't see his erection stirring.

'I know you feel responsible for protecting me, but you're not my keeper. I choose who I share myself with.'

That airy wave of her hand would be more impressive if she hadn't been a virgin thirty minutes ago.

And if he didn't feel such a strong connection to her. Not just to a memory of the girl she'd once been, but to Lola, the woman he'd begun to know in recent days. The woman who intrigued, tempted and disturbed him.

With her he was alternately out of his depth or attuned at a gut-deep level that didn't require explanation or conversation between them. Both worried him.

Niall mightn't be her keeper but nor was he some passing stranger.

'Yet you didn't choose to share yourself with anyone until tonight. Why is that?'

Lola gnawed the corner of her mouth, a habit

she'd had as a kid when nervous or cornered in an argument. 'I've been busy and the time never seemed right.'

Niall surveyed her minutely, knowing there was something she wasn't saying. Sensing it was something he needed to know. He was about to press her then paused.

Who did he think he was? The virginity police?

Was it really his business why she hadn't had sex before?

Like a searing streak of lightning, realisation hit. *He was glad he was the first.* Even if it did make him feel ridiculously possessive. Ants crawled beneath his skin at the idea of Lola doing with anyone else what she'd done with him.

He told himself he should be grateful Lola was okay, taking it in her stride. Almost as if it were just another holiday experience to tick off her list, like attending a glitzy party.

Niall frowned. Was that what had happened? Was he a passing diversion, helping to turn her enforced seclusion into a fun break?

He was stunned by the white-hot blast of rejection he felt at the idea. And the swift urge to close the space between them and claim her, imprinting himself in her pores, in every nerve and pleasure receptor in her body. So that in future, whenever Lola thought of desire and sexual delight, she thought of him.

Why? It wasn't as if he wanted her imagining tonight was anything more than an overflow of pent-up sexual frustration. Imagine if Lola, like some previous lovers, started thinking in terms of a long-term relationship, wedding bells and families!

That doused the stirring heat in his groin as if he'd dived under an iceberg.

Because the one thing Niall could never do was become a family man. The thought of being responsible for a wife and kids stirred old nausea in his gut and dark shadows in his mind.

'Are you okay, Niall?'

He grimaced. 'I'm the one who should ask that.' He'd never been with a virgin. He didn't know what he'd expected. Blood and tears? 'Are you sure I didn't hurt you?'

Again she chewed her lip. Niall wanted to lean in and stop her, kissing her mouth into ripe softness before plundering her sweetness. He shuddered and tried to rein in his galloping imagination.

'Briefly. So briefly I barely noticed.'

Yet the wash of pink covering her breasts, throat and cheeks was a reminder of how new this was to her. It made him want to beat his chest in primitive triumph at being her only lover. Or hang his head in shame at betraying the trust she and her family had placed in him. The betrayal of his own code of conduct. Sex with a woman under his protection, a vulnerable woman in hiding.

'In fact...' She paused, slanting him a look under

long, veiling eyelashes that he felt as a tightening in his groin. 'I feel so good, I'd like to do it again.'

'Again?'

Tomorrow. She meant tomorrow or maybe the day after. When she was no longer tender—

'It's not that odd, surely.' Her attention dropped to somewhere around his collarbone, the pink on her cheeks deepening to rose. 'But maybe it's too soon for you. Do you need more time?'

As if he weren't fighting a losing battle against arousal! He pressed his lips into a flat line, rather than blurt out the truth.

She looked adorably hesitant and devastatingly provocative. Everything from the dark curve of her long eyelashes to those reddened lips to her luscious body beneath the water called to him.

Her chin hiked up but still she didn't meet his eyes. 'But I'll understand if you don't want to. If you prefer more experienced partners.'

Niall opened his mouth to tell her it wasn't a matter of experience, and that it wouldn't happen again. Because he wasn't right for her on so many levels.

Even if it would be torture, holding back.

Shock grabbed him by the throat when he heard himself say in a gravel voice, 'You're the sexiest woman I've ever known, Lola. That's why I stayed here and showered. Because I worried if I went back to the bedroom I'd persuade you into sex again when you need time to recover.'

It was a relief to unleash the truth. Despite the

self-disgust stirring in his belly. But he was only human, and resisting Lola, naked, enticing Lola, was futile.

Already he was on his feet beside the bath, towering over her.

Yet she was the one with the power. Her wide-eyed stare at his erection set his body flaming. It was an effort not to leap into that massive tub with her and drive himself hard between her thighs. She reduced him to raw, unvarnished hunger, stripped of finesse. It was a frightening experience for a man used to controlling his life, his environment, and his libido.

'I'm so glad,' she murmured, kneeling at the edge of the bath.

Niall was bending forward to help her up and into his arms when she planted her wet palm on his thigh, another on his bare buttock, and leaned in, delicately touching the tip of his arousal with her tongue.

Arrows of fire scorched their flaming way through his body. He froze, his body refusing to step away and the voice in his head telling him only a fool would deny her.

Serious as an owl, her forehead furrowed in concentration, she touched him again, this time bending lower and laving right along his length.

A shudder buckled his knees yet stiffened his sinews. He found his hands clutching at her dark hair.

Niall swallowed, the sensation like the scrape of

shattered glass. He croaked, 'You don't have to do that.' Maybe she thought it was expected, since he'd gone down on her. Yet instead of gently pushing her away, he held her where she was.

'I want to. I'm curious.' Another lingering lick, this time ending with her lips drawing on him, and he shuddered.

Sensations bombarded Lola, delicious sensations. The taste of Niall, spice and salt. The inferno heat of him against her face. The texture of silk over his iron-hard erection that was unlike anything else. She lifted her hand from his thigh, tentatively circling her fingers around him, and he pressed forward into her caress. She caught a groan over the rush of her pulse in her ears.

Then there was the taut muscle of his backside, trembling and bunching beneath her hand, more proof that Niall was no longer in charge.

The thought excited her. Aroused her. Heat forked in a fiery slipstream from her breasts to her belly, to that needy place inside where only Niall had been. Where she wanted him again.

Slowly, carefully, she leaned closer, drawing him in. She was rewarded with a hiss of shock from Niall and a buck of his hips, pushing deeper, demanding.

Lola paused, despite her excitement, a little stunned by his raw response, the desperate way he thrust against her and the way his hands held her captive.

He was so big, so strong. She was at the mercy of that strength.

Except, looking up through slitted eyes, she saw Niall watching her, his face pared back to lines of stark arousal. That was when she registered the tremor in his hands and the lost look in those remarkable eyes.

Slowly she drew on his engorged flesh, delighting in his heavy shudder. His head dropped back, his mouth open on a gasp that told her it was the other way around. Niall was at her mercy.

Carefully, alert to his responses, she slid her hand along him, squeezing a little, learning from each jolt and sigh what he liked.

And what he liked, she did too. Lola felt privileged and powerful, bringing this strong, ardent man, if not to his knees, then to a point of shaking neediness. She wanted—

Firm hands moved her back. Glittering eyes held hers as he tilted her chin up.

'Later.' His voice ground low and husky, but there was no mistaking who was taking the lead now.

Lola considered protesting. She had a lot more experimenting and exploring to do. But something in Niall's heated stare told her she wouldn't regret it.

'Is that a promise?'

Niall's sudden bark of laughter made her smile.

'If you think I'd try to prevent you you've got rocks in your head. But right now there's something

I want more.' The smile on his lips turned hungry. 'You, Lola.'

He stepped back, ransacking the cupboards and finally pulling out a box of condoms.

'Shall we?' Sheathed, he held out his arm to help her out of the bath.

Instead Lola eased back away from him, supremely conscious of the warm water eddying around her sensitised flesh. 'Why don't you join me? There's lots of room.' The bath was constructed on a decadently generous size.

For one beat of her heart Niall paused. Then he lifted those long legs over the side and sank down, arms splaying out along the rim of the bath. He leaned his head back, watching her with dark, beckoning eyes, like some sybaritic pasha, eyeing a favourite concubine.

Lola blinked. Clearly she'd kept a lid on her sexuality for too long, judging by tonight's surprising impulses and imaginings.

'What are you thinking, Lola?'

She moved nearer, reading the rapid tic of his pulse at his throat and the lines of taut tendons and bunched muscles. It cost Niall to appear relaxed.

He wanted her. Niall Pedersen, the man she'd fantasised about for years, wanted her that badly.

'I'm thinking sleep is overrated.'

His arm snaked out, long fingers taking hers and drawing her to him. Lola expected him to reverse their positions so she sat against the end of the bath. Instead he planted his hands on her hips and pulled her across him, his erection bobbing against her belly.

A twist of need spiralled through her.

'On your knees, Lola. Hands on my shoulders.' With the words he nudged her legs open so she straddled him, knees tucked behind his hips.

Long fingers parting the flesh between her thighs made her hiss and slide against him.

'You *are* eager.' But he didn't sound smug, more relieved. 'How about we go at your pace this time, sweetheart?'

Lola nodded yet hesitated, not quite sure.

Then Niall smiled. The sort of smile that dug right down under her heart and squeezed. His hands went again to her hips, gently tugging her up onto her knees.

'Now, gently down.' His hand was there, and something else, nudging her.

A tiny movement and she felt pressure, delicious pressure. Another movement and Niall grimaced, his fingers branding her hips but she didn't mind because everything felt so perfect. Shuffling a little further forward, she let herself sink, let her breasts slide against his hard chest as their bodies melded.

The sensations were an intense variation on what had gone before. Exquisite fullness, sensitivity that bordered between pleasure and something even more intense.

But best of all wasn't the physical, it was, again,

the feeling of oneness. Niall's gaze held hers, infinitely gentle, infinitely hot, as he urged her back up and she sank down again, faster, harder.

Excitement shuddered through her.

Niall's hands went to her breasts and her breath seized. She leaned in, and one big hand cupped the back of her head, bringing her down for a slow, open-mouthed kiss that was all the more erotic because it imitated their bodies mating.

Lola clutched Niall's damp hair, holding him still as the kiss deepened and her rhythm quickened. Kaleidoscope sparks fizzed in her blood and flickered behind her closed eyelids. Then Niall held her to him as he thrust up, pinioning her, groaning her name, and the world shattered.

As she came spinning slowly back to earth, dazed and not sure where she ended and he began, Niall cradled her close. She sank against him, spent and exhausted, knowing there was nowhere on earth she'd prefer to be.

That was when full realisation hit and she understood the appalling fix she was in.

She'd told herself reality could never measure up to the idealised man she'd built in her head. Now she learned that real life Niall far outstripped her fantasies. Making love with him felt...

That was just it. Even she, newly inducted into the mysteries of sex, understood her euphoria wasn't just about spectacular physical gratification.

It was as much about how she felt, emotionally.

Because her crush on him hadn't merely survived the years of separation.

It had grown and expanded.

Into love.

Her breath snagged.

She'd made mistakes in her life. Was this the biggest yet?

What on earth was she going to do?

CHAPTER ELEVEN

NEXT MORNING NIALL found the resolve to leave the bed before dawn and go for a long run on the beach, rather than wake Lola for sex. Then, after checking she was still asleep, he showered in another bathroom and went out to buy their breakfast.

He should have been pleased when he got back to find her up and dressed, because in theory it made it easier to keep his distance. No matter how enthusiastic she'd been, he was pretty certain she'd be sore this morning.

Plus his conscience was finally working, reminding him of all the reasons Lola was taboo.

Should have been taboo.

A pity his body didn't get the message. Just looking at Lola aroused him. And Lola in that slinky dress was torture to a sinner who'd already crossed from right to wrong and wanted to indulge himself again.

If Lola had given him the slightest encouragement...

But she hadn't. Today she'd been different. Self-contained.

She'd eaten a hearty breakfast and said what a good time she'd had at the party. For a second her eyes had glowed with warmth and he'd wanted to wrap his arms around her and hold her close. Even if they didn't have sex, he wanted to hold her. His arms felt empty this morning. He'd never before experienced an ache for one particular woman.

He'd watched her mouth as she sipped her coffee and chewed on a pastry and remembered those lips on his. And on other parts of his body. Want had turned to blazing, biting hunger. If she'd given any hint she desired him again…

Instead she'd worried about getting back to her computer and her job. As if what they'd shared had been fun but forgettable.

Niall hadn't been sure what to expect but it wasn't that. She'd pulled the rug from under him in more ways than he could count.

He couldn't even complain that she treated him with easy-going friendship when for days he'd been trying to do the same.

Now, in his study, back on the mountain, Niall felt that familiar tremor of need. It hadn't abated one bit, though he'd worked all day to repress his lust.

Which was the right thing to do. Belatedly.

Especially as Lola had kept her distance all day. There'd been no flirting. No eager invitation back to bed.

Niall had learned that though she was inexperienced, Lola wasn't shy about sexual desire. She was generous and demanding, not afraid to ask for what she wanted, or to give.

Another shudder racked him as he remembered how wholeheartedly she gave.

Inevitably Niall's gaze lifted from the computer screen he'd stared at blankly to Lola, set up in a shady spot next to the pool with her laptop.

It was late afternoon and she'd been for a lunchtime swim. Instead of dressing fully again, she'd spent the afternoon wearing a work shirt over that skimpy bikini.

From the waist up she looked all business for her online meetings.

But from there down she was tantalising temptation. The streamlined curves of her calves, thighs and hips mesmerised him, killing his ability to concentrate.

Shut in his study, Niall had got no work done, apart from checking fruitlessly for news of Braithwaite. He'd spent half the afternoon imagining being naked with Lola and the other half watching her through the window or finding excuses to talk with her. He'd made them a salad lunch. Then coffee. He'd shared the update his Melbourne staff had provided, that there'd been no sign of Braithwaite at her flat. Lola had reciprocated with a similar update from the police.

That had sent Niall back to his study where he'd

spent an hour scoping further options to draw her stalker out, discussing them with experts, and going back to the drawing board.

Now she was smiling as she talked with someone online. A man or a woman? Threads of jealousy that he had no right to feel wove through him, tangling in a knot in his belly.

What the hell was happening to him?

He'd never expected any woman's undivided attention, except in bed.

Niall shoved his chair back from the desk and paced the room, trying to wrangle his thoughts into line.

He'd been ready this morning to tell Lola the sex had been terrific but couldn't happen again. Not just because she was Ed's sister and he was responsible for her safety. But because he knew, deep in his bones, that Lola wasn't a woman for a short affair. She was a woman for keeps. One who deserved a solid, loving relationship. The sort of relationship he simply couldn't provide.

Niall wasn't arrogant enough to think she'd want that with him. She'd made it clear she was enjoying the chance for sexual experimentation. But he couldn't take the chance of blurring the lines between them. Not when it could mean hurting her.

But she'd undercut him, treating him with the easy familiarity of an old friend, all trace of the lover gone.

He should be grateful.

He should be pleased.

Instead he was wound so tight with frustration and pique he didn't know what to do with himself.

Except take his lead from her and be what she wanted, an old friend.

Even if it killed him.

'Stir-fry okay for dinner?'

Lola looked up from her laptop to find Niall, seriously scrumptious in a black polo shirt and pale cotton trousers, standing in the doorway. Her insides gave an all too familiar shimmy and she had to work at sitting still and not throwing herself into his arms.

Powerful arms that had held her safe when the world shattered in a fire burst of ecstasy and her heart welled with all the emotion she couldn't dare share with him.

'That sounds great. Can I help?'

It wasn't as if she'd achieve anything here. It was late and she'd only kept the computer open, trying to work, because the alternative was to do something stupid like fling herself at the man who'd avoided her all day.

He couldn't have made it clearer that last night had been, if not a mistake, then a one-off.

He'd left her in the early hours, while it was still pitch dark, presumably to sleep in another room. That had extinguished her glow of well-being and put an end to her sleepy musings about a lazy morning in bed. Forget any hopes Niall would consider an affair, even just for the length of her stay in Queensland.

Disappointment had seared through her. Last night had been remarkable. Astounding.

Her heart dived.

The only intimacy she'd ever share with the man she loved.

How naïve she'd been to think he couldn't hurt her more than he already had.

She'd spent the day acting as if it hadn't happened. As if they were just old friends. It was the only way she knew to salvage her pride and stop herself from doing something stupid like kissing him.

He'd only reject her again.

'It's fine. I'll manage.'

Lola closed the laptop and rose, pinning on a smile. She was stiff from sitting for hours. That was why she moved. Not to be closer to Niall.

'It'll be easier with two.'

Because, despite everything, she couldn't stay away. Her weakness for this man ran blood deep.

What would it hurt to indulge herself and be near him? He wasn't going to bridge the chasm between them. She'd only be here another couple of days. After that she mightn't see Niall again.

Lola ignored the sudden ache in her middle and concentrated on trying to look relaxed.

It was only as she followed him into the beautifully appointed chef's kitchen that she realised he wasn't relaxed either. His shoulders sat high and his hands were bunched at his sides.

'Is something wrong, Niall? Do you need to get back to Brisbane?' He'd only come here because of her. 'You don't need to stay and chaperone me. I'll be fine alone.'

Lola faltered as he swung around to face her. To her surprise she read something like anger in his strong features. Banked heat in his eyes and re-pressed emotion in the taut line of his lips.

Energy ripped through her in a jagged strike, like lightning hitting earth. Her whole body vibrated, her fingertips tingling.

No, not anger. Not totally.

'Eager to be rid of me, are you, Lola?' His jaw firmed. His arms folded over his chest, muscles bulging and rippling beneath dark gold skin. 'Am I cramping your style? If I left you could invite Jake Sinclair here. Or would you rather have the pass-code to the Gold Coast apartment? That might be more convenient.'

Lola frowned up at him, her hand planted on the vast granite-topped island bench for support. For suddenly her head felt swimmy. Or maybe it was her knees.

'Niall? What are you talking about? Why would I invite Jake Sinclair here?'

His gaze locked on hers, not dark navy but bright cobalt. How could a cool colour look so hot?

He blinked and his expression changed. A tremor passed through him and Lola watched his shoulders drop, his fingers stretch as he unfolded his arms.

For the first time she could remember Niall seemed reluctant to meet her eyes. Instead he stared past her, as if the kitchen cabinetry held him enthralled.

'Sorry.' He shook his head, then raked his fingers through his hair. 'Ignore me, I'm talking nonsense. It's not been a good day. I shouldn't take it out on you.'

He moved towards the refrigerator but her hand on his arm stopped him.

In slow motion he tilted his head down to stare at her fingers, as if no one had ever had the temerity to touch him.

Lola told herself to drop her hand but instead her fingers gripped harder, digging into taut, hot flesh, its smattering of dark hair tickling.

She was about to ask if she'd done something wrong when her synapses fired and she made sense of his words.

'You think I have an assignation with Jake Sinclair?' The idea was ludicrous, but she read the truth in Niall's face.

Now she had no trouble yanking her hand away. She cradled it against herself as if stung.

'What are you saying, Niall? That I planned a sexual liaison last night with a man I'd never met before?' She hefted a quick breath but still felt short of oxygen. 'Right before I spent the night with you?' The words rushed out, so fast they tripped over each other.

She backed up a step, her mouth crumpling at the horrible, sour taste on her tongue.

'Lola, no! I don't. It's not like that!'

No trace of anger on his face now. Niall looked as if she'd kneed him in the groin, his face a strange pasty colour. She wished she *had* kneed him in the groin. Instead she'd spent the day daydreaming about making love with him!

'Or do you believe sex with you magically turned me from virgin to vamp? That I'm now so desperate for sex I'd ring up a virtual stranger and offer myself to him?'

Red mist filled her vision. What they'd shared last night had felt special, transcendent even. Niall's words made it seem tawdry.

'No!' Hard hands grabbed her above the elbows. 'Of course not!'

'You know,' she said, spurred by hurt and fury, 'it's not a bad idea. I liked sex.' *With Niall!* But she ignored that scream of outrage in her head. 'Why don't you go to Brisbane and I might consider calling Jake?'

She didn't hear what Niall said. Or she heard but couldn't make sense of the growling undercurrent of oaths over the thrumming of her pulse.

But she saw the fierce light in his eyes. A light

so savage it made every cell in her body tingle with dangerous excitement.

'You won't call him.' Niall ground the words out with slow emphasis. 'Not for sex.'

Lola had never tossed her head in her life. She did now. 'I can do whatever I like. *Be* with anyone I like.'

Niall inclined his head. 'But you want to be with *me*, don't you, Lola?' His gaze challenged and she couldn't look away.

Did she imagine desperation in those stark features? Surely not.

Niall trailed the tip of his index finger across her open lips then down, by torturously slow degrees, to her throat, her collarbone, the open collar of her shirt, lingering there, just above where her heart thundered.

Exquisite sensations bombarded her. She was torn between wanting to slap his hand away and hooking it into her shirt so he could rip it open.

'Why should I want a man who thinks I'm…?' Words failed her.

'I don't. Of course I don't. I took out my frustration on you. I'm sorry.' His palm flattened on the upper slope of her chest and she felt it like a brand of possession. 'I've spent the day going crazy, keeping my distance because it's the right thing to do. When all I want is to be buried deep inside you, feeling you climax around me.'

Shock smacked her.

'You want me? You're…jealous? There's nothing to be jealous of!'

'Pathetic, isn't it? I know you haven't got a thing with Jake. I don't know where the words came from. It was a despicable thing to say and I only did it because I'm in a foul mood. I apologise.' Niall slid his hand up, back to her face, but this time he cradled her cheek with infinite tenderness, his own features rigid with what looked like pain.

Lola had never seen him hurt like this. Never known him to lash out.

'I want you, so badly,' he admitted. 'I know I shouldn't. I know all the reasons I need to keep my distance. All the reasons I'm wrong for you. But they don't help.' He sucked in air like a drowning man about to go under. 'So tell me that you despise me, and I'll walk away.'

'And if I don't?'

The world stilled, her heartbeat slowing as, amazed, she read vulnerability in Niall's proud features. Regret, shame and arousal.

For about a second Lola contemplated stepping away. Making good on her self-talk about severing the bond with Niall.

But after last night it was impossible. Especially now when she saw pain in his eyes.

As a teenager, Niall had been reckless of his safety but he'd never come close to hurting her. She'd have taken her oath that he'd do anything rather than harm her.

He might not love her but he cared for her. And he wanted her. He looked tortured. Whether by the fact he'd hurt her or by the force of his desire, or both, Lola couldn't tell.

She strove for pride but couldn't hold it. She loved him so much she'd take what she could get.

Lola took his hand and placed it on her breast, rejoicing in his hissed intake of breath and the convulsive way his hand tightened, making pleasure sing through her.

'Really?' He shook his head. 'After what I said you should—'

Lola put her hand over his mouth. 'I'll decide what I should and shouldn't do.'

He opened his mouth against her hand and licked her palm, slowly, as he gently squeezed her breast. A shaft of glowing heat tunnelled down to her pelvis, making her shake.

Niall gathered her close and she was never more grateful for his strength.

It was wonderful to discover he shook too.

Lola moistened her dry lips and stood on her toes to whisper against his ear. 'What I want, Niall, is you buried deep inside me, so you can feel me climax around you and I can feel you.' She felt him jolt with surprise, and triumph slashed through her. Emboldened, she nipped his earlobe. 'And I want it now.'

Instantly Niall spanned her hips with his capable

hands and lifted her up onto the island bench, pushing her knees wide.

Dark eyes held hers.

'You're sure?' He sounded gruff, as if the words stuck in his throat. Lola understood the feeling. She didn't even try to speak, just nodded, watching his mouth curl in a slow, sexy grin that turned her to mush.

'I love a woman who knows what she wants.'

Love. For a second her thoughts snagged on the word. Except Niall slid his hand down inside the front of her bikini bottom, fingers carefully yet ruthlessly probing, and Lola forgot about everything but the need for more.

She wasn't just damp there, she was wet, and the slide of his hand...

'Niall! Please.'

She shoved the fabric down her hips, wriggling to free herself, while he pulled his hand away and reached into his pocket.

Her eyes rounded as he lifted a foil package and tore it with his teeth.

Seeing her expression, he smiled grimly. 'No, I don't usually carry condoms wherever I go. But today I hoped...' He shook his head. 'I shouldn't. I kept telling myself you need space. But you undo me, Lola.'

The idea that she messed with his head appealed. It evened up things between them because that was exactly what he did to her.

She smiled and pressed a light kiss to his lips. Niall caught her to him and turned it into something long and soul deep. Her body was on fire for him but so was her heart.

When they pulled apart, gasping for air, Niall shucked his trousers and underwear and put on the condom. Seconds later they were both naked.

Niall ate her up with glazed eyes. 'One day we're going to take our time, Lola. We might even do something unconventional like start making love in bed.'

It was a tiny thing, but her heart sang at the implication they'd do this again. That this wasn't, after all, a one-night thing.

She reached for his shoulders. 'But not now.'

'Definitely not now.' He positioned himself between her spread thighs.

For the longest moment they were still, staring into each other's eyes, absorbing the feel of their bodies just touching, and the anticipation shimmering between them. Then, with one slow, smooth movement, Niall pushed home, right to the heart of her.

Her mouth fell open on a gasp of astonishment. She'd learned what to expect last night yet this felt so profound. With his grave gaze pinioning hers, his heavy grip holding her in a way that was both possessive and caressing, it was easy to believe Niall too experienced more than sexual arousal. That he also felt the emotional bond.

But inevitably arousal won.

Lola grabbed his shoulders as he leaned forward till she lay back on the cool countertop. His bare chest covered her breasts and she arched as his chest hair tickled her.

Niall urged her legs up high over his hips, sinking even deeper, and Lola welcomed him with a circle of her hips and a squeeze of muscles that made him judder.

Then there was no time for thought, just the quick tempo of their bodies rising and joining, the rhythm that became a runaway pulse, urgent and deep. More urgent. Deeper. Quicker. Hungry and hungrier. Her fingernails scored his smooth shoulders and he responded with a powerful thrust that seated him impossibly tight as stars burst and they climaxed together, clinging, eyes locked and, she'd swear, hearts pounding in tandem.

Ages later, when the world came back, Niall gathered her close and carried her to his bedroom. No words were spoken. Lola wasn't sure she was capable of speech. Besides, their bodies spoke for them.

He didn't let her go, even getting into the bed he cradled her near and she revelled in the bond between them.

For the rest of the night there was barely a moment when Niall wasn't touching her. Either making love, or just holding her.

They remembered to eat around midnight, but only on snacks they fed to each other. That turned out to be deliciously messy, necessitating a long soak in the bath till the water turned cold and their flesh pruny, and Niall insisted she needed sleep. They slept tangled together, then saw the dawn in making love again.

Lola knew, whatever happened in the future, she had this one night of profound joy to treasure.

The question was, could she have more?

CHAPTER TWELVE

THE ANSWER WAS YES. She could have more.

Because after that night things changed.

Niall never spoke about keeping his distance or her family's expectations. He was with her all the time, except for the hours they both worked.

They got into a routine, each working in their own part of the sprawling house, totally alone but for the housekeeper who appeared every couple of days to clean and bring supplies. Lola and Niall did everything together, eating, bathing, swimming, sleeping.

Not sleeping.

Her mouth tugged into a reminiscent smile as she thought of the hours they'd spent last night, making love.

They should both be too exhausted to work, given how little sleep they got. Instead Lola seemed to fizz with energy. When she did sleep, inevitably in Niall's arms, it was a deep, restful slumber that left her feeling rejuvenated.

As for the rest, work was going surprisingly well,

despite her being isolated from colleagues, and her relationship with Niall had grown into something new. It wasn't just sexual attraction. The easy intimacy they'd had years ago was back, but coloured by a new awareness and respect.

It was over two weeks since they'd arrived here and their relationship had grown into the give and take of a well-matched couple.

It surprised her how fast and easily they'd become a couple in much more than sex. Maybe their history together, the fact that they'd known each other so well for so long, was part of it.

Lola knew who Niall was at heart, his strengths, like determination, generosity and kindness, and his weaknesses, like keeping problems to himself and automatically taking charge. The latter, at least, she saw changing as he stopped trying to manage her.

She reached for her coffee and sipped. The only dark cloud was the fact Braithwaite was still at large. There'd been no further attacks on her home and it looked unlikely the police would prove anything against him.

Lola dreaded returning to Melbourne. Partly because it meant facing Braithwaite. She wasn't optimistic or naïve enough to believe her tormentor had seen the error of his ways and decided to leave her alone. More likely he'd sussed that the woman in her flat wasn't Lola, and he was biding his time.

But what she really fretted over was leaving Niall, whose home and business were here in Queensland.

What they shared was more than a fling. She *hoped* they had a future together. It felt that was where they were headed. And yet...

She looked up from her coffee cup. Niall was shaking hands with the business acquaintance he'd spotted in the doorway of the elegant restaurant. It seemed they were saying goodbye.

He turned back into the dining room, heading for their lunch table. He didn't seem to notice the eager looks turned his way or the whispered comments. Instead his gaze was fixed on her with devastating intensity.

A woman could get used to Niall looking at her that way, disregarding every other woman, including quite a few beautiful blondes, like the sort she'd seen him with in press reports.

'Is everything all right, Lola?' He pulled out his chair and sat, immediately reaching for her hand. She loved the way Niall touched her frequently. Those tiny, tender caresses that spoke not just of sex, but of caring. 'You looked pensive.'

'Did I?'

Niall watched her straighten, her mouth curving into a smile that looked, not wary precisely, but not as easy and open as usual.

He'd grown accustomed to her open pleasure in everything they shared, from cooking to discussing business trends or books. From watching a movie, snuggled up together, to sex.

He wasn't just accustomed but hooked. He could no more keep away from Lola than he could walk on the waves that lapped the beach outside.

Even knowing this was wrong. That in the long run, he couldn't be the man for her.

Niall's penance was the torture of knowing this must end. Lola deserved better than him. He should never have touched her.

With luck she'd tire of him soon. Realise he wasn't the sort of man she should waste her time on and move on. Though the thought filled him with dread. He wasn't ready to say goodbye to sweet, sassy Lola, her seriousness and her sexy ways.

'Were you thinking about Braithwaite?' He rubbed his thumb over her wrist, noting its heavy throb. 'I'm sure there'll be news soon. We just have to be patient.'

It frustrated him, the way her stalker had dropped under the radar. Naturally Braithwaite had backed off when his spy camera was found. But sooner or later he'd try something again, and the police and Pedersen Security would be waiting for him.

'I know. But for how long? Three weeks? Three months?' Lola looked at their clasped hands, her mouth flattened. 'I'm in limbo. It feels like Braithwaite has won, driving me from my home, disrupting my life.'

Pressure built in Niall's chest. 'I know it feels like that at the moment but, believe me, we'll put an end to his harassment.' Niall and his team were pursuing every avenue to make that happen. 'But there are compensations.'

A moment ago he was thinking about how it would be best if Lola left him. Yet he couldn't bear to think of her unhappy here. 'Your work's going well, isn't it? It sounds like the new project is really progressing.' He offered a winning smile. 'And this isn't a bad place for a break.'

Surely it wasn't just the place, but the company too, that she enjoyed. But Niall refused to fish for compliments.

He *knew* Lola was happy here with him. He'd felt it, seen it in her smiles and enthusiasm. Read it in their avid sex life, but more, in the contentment and ease that had grown between them.

He'd never experienced anything like it. A unique and stimulating combination of full-on sexual attraction that showed no signs of abating, melded with friendship and a level of understanding that sometimes made words superfluous because they were so attuned.

'Not a bad place at all.' She smiled and Niall felt the unfamiliar tightness behind his ribs ease. 'Sometimes I wish we could continue like this for ever.' Her eyes locked on his and a fizz of intense pleasure filled him.

Till reality, that cold, unwelcome guest at the table, muscled its way in again.

There could be no for ever for them.

He could give Lola what she needed for now but

she was too precious, too special to waste on someone like him long term.

He drew in a sharp breath to match the sharp pain lancing his lungs.

That was his punishment for breaking the rules and giving in to his lust for her. Even now the clock was ticking.

'The best holidays are like that, aren't they? You want them to continue indefinitely.' He managed to sound upbeat but couldn't summon a smile this time.

No matter how right and sensible, he wasn't ready for this interlude to end. Inevitably it must, but every instinct screamed *not yet*!

Which was why he forced himself to continue. 'But even Paradise would pall after a while, don't you think?'

Lola tilted her head in that assessing way she'd always had.

Sometimes it felt as if she saw deeper inside him than anyone ever had. Further than the business competitors who searched for his weak points. Deeper than the father he hadn't seen in years. His dad had seen the bleak, damning darkness inside Niall and he'd chosen to turn away, focusing his energy on his new family, pretending his first son didn't exist.

Who could blame him?

'Niall? Did you hear me?'

Lola leaned close, looking concerned.

He sat straighter, giving her a smile that he hoped covered his disturbing thoughts.

But he was shocked at the force of those thoughts. The piercing regret that he couldn't be the man for Lola. And the suspicion Lola saw at least a little of his inner turmoil. Niall had spent years masking that, in his teens behind an overtly don't-care attitude and as an adult with rigid self-discipline.

Looking into those warm, hazel eyes, Niall felt his self-discipline waver.

'Sorry, I missed that.'

'I asked if there was time for a walk on the beach before we head back to your house. I know we spent the morning in the surf, but the weather's perfect.'

He smiled. He loved the fact Lola was just as enthusiastic about a walk by the sea, or seeing brightly coloured birds up close, as she was about attending a glittering society party or being superlative at her job. She made him appreciate pleasures he often took for granted in his high-demand, high-profile world.

'Whatever you like, Lola.'

Her eyes danced wickedly and she leaned in, her summery scent teasing him. 'Well…there's something else I'd like to do, but we need privacy.' Instantly Niall's libido revved into life. 'We can do that when we get home,' she purred as she rose from the table.

For a second he basked in a glow of well-being. The sensual promise of her words and suggestive glance, the way she referred to his place as *home*. As if it could eventually be more than a place to retreat for brief periods. As if together they could——

Niall clamped down a barrier against such thoughts. A shared future was impossible.

He'd have to settle for what they had now, enjoy it to the full, because, he realised with shocking clarity, it was probably the best he'd ever have.

'Niall?' She paused, looking back over her shoulder. 'Are you okay?'

Lola didn't know his secrets but she had an uncanny ability to read his mood. Something he'd do well to remember.

'Never better, lover.' He put his arm around her on the pretext of guiding her from the plush restaurant. In reality he was determined not to miss a moment of touching her.

Leaving their shoes in the car, they strolled along the beach, down on the wet, white sand, where shallow waves curled around their ankles. By mutual consent they headed away from the red and yellow flags marking the safe swimming zone.

Hands linked, they didn't talk much. It was enough to enjoy the beach, the day and the company. Lola skipped, yelping, when a higher waved raced in, splashing her skirt, and Niall swung her up into his arms, revelling in the simple pleasure of holding her.

'Swing me too?'

At first Niall didn't know where the voice came

from. He was too attuned to Lola's laugh and her blinding smile. Then he felt something touch his leg and looked down.

There, her hand on his knee, was a little girl, auburn curls dancing in the breeze, dark eyes turned up to him.

'Please, mister. Me too?'

Niall's breath backed up.

The little hand patted his leg and a hopeful smile filled her face.

Niall found his breath and expelled it in an audible whoosh. For a second the resemblance had been uncanny, but now he saw the differences between that eager face and the one he'd known.

Yet pain still knifed his chest.

Slowly he moved away a step, then another, till he could put Lola down on dry sand.

The child followed. He turned his head. Where were her parents?

'Swing me, please?'

Niall shook his head, telling himself no parent would want a stranger, especially a male stranger, cuddling their little girl.

From the corner of his eye he saw Lola shoot him a look. Then she crouched down in front of the child. 'Hello, my name's Lola. What's yours?'

The girl shook her head. 'I'm not allowed to talk to strangers.'

That almost jerked a laugh from Niall's frozen vocal cords. She couldn't talk to Lola but she could beg him to swing her through the air? Her parents had their hands full getting the stranger danger message through to this little one.

'Where's your family?' Lola persisted. 'They might be worried about you.'

Niall scanned the family groups scattered along the beach. None seemed to be frantically searching for a lost child.

He felt again that little hand paw his leg and flinched.

'Plee-ee-ase?'

She was a cute little thing and he saw the soft light in Lola's eyes. Did she want kids? The idea stabbed him.

'No swings unless your parents say so.'

His words emerged brusquely but they had their effect. Seconds later the child was racing up the beach to where a woman was busy helping two other children built a giant sandcastle.

Even from a distance Niall saw her shock as she registered the little girl race towards her, pointing back to them. The shock of someone who hadn't realised their charge was in potential danger.

Something rippled deep in the icy depths of his belly and curled around the back of his neck. Fellow feeling.

Beside him, Lola waved her hand and the woman acknowledged it with a nod as she gathered the child close.

Seconds later they heard a wail. Not of pain but frustration. Clearly the girl's mother had said *no*.

Relief settled in Niall's belly as he clasped Lola's hand. They turned back the way they'd come.

Lola slanted a look at him and shook her head. 'She'll keep her mum busy.'

'But you liked her.'

'She has character. Don't you think?'

Niall shrugged. 'I'm no expert on kids.'

'No.' He sensed her gaze on him. 'You didn't seem comfortable. Haven't you been around children at all?'

The ice inside spread, crackling up his spine, making him shudder. 'Only a bit.'

Liar. But that was way in the past. A past he tried never to visit.

'I spent years getting extra money babysitting. I enjoyed it.'

Niall slanted a look at her. 'You'd be good at it.' She had the patience and focus. And a great sense of humour. He could imagine her on her hands and knees, playing games with the kids she looked after.

'I'm sure you will be when the time comes.'

'Sorry?'

She turned away, apparently fascinated by a board rider. 'If or when you have children.'

Familiar coldness blanketed his shoulders, despite the bright sunlight. 'That's not going to happen. I won't ever have a family. You know I'm a loner.'

* * *

Lola couldn't get Niall's words out of her head. It wasn't just the words but how he'd said them. With such iron-clad certainty. Each word hard and definite. As if he could know for sure what the future held.

For some reason the joy went out of the day.

She tried to tell herself Niall didn't mean it about never having family, and always being alone. But she couldn't convince herself.

On the way back up the mountain, conversation was desultory and Niall left her almost immediately after they arrived, saying he needed to return a call. Lola had taken a call herself, from the police, saying Braithwaite had been spotted near her home and that they were hopeful he might be planning something that would incriminate him.

The news didn't cheer her. Her thoughts kept circling back to Niall and those dismissive words.

She'd spent years pining for this man. Now she'd made the mistake of falling in love with him.

Bad enough that there was a huge gulf between them. They moved in completely different circles as well as living in different states. If he truly believed he'd face the future alone, that meant he saw this as a short fling without a chance of it becoming something else. The idea caught at her ribs, stymying her breathing.

She wanted that chance.

Wanted a future with Niall.

Which was why she couldn't let it rest. She rapped on the door to his study and pushed it open. He stood looking out at the gathering dusk, birds wheeling over the trees in a swirl of colour.

'Niall...'

'Lola.' He swung around and she tensed. His expression didn't bode well.

'I wondered if you wanted dinner soon.' Coward! But suddenly she wasn't sure she wanted to know if he'd been serious about being a loner. About how he saw their relationship or whether there was any tiny chance in the future of him returning her feelings.

'In a while.' He paused and she saw his chest rise with a deep breath. As if he too girded himself for bad news. 'I wanted to talk with you. It's important.'

She didn't like the sound of that. Yet she needed to know. So she crossed the room, let him take her hand and pull her down to sit on the long leather sofa beside him.

Yesterday they'd made love here. They'd still been wet from the pool and they'd laughed as the leather squeaked against their slick, bare skin. Until rapture took them and they'd lost themselves in each other.

Their body language was different now, despite their clasped hands resting on Niall's thigh. There was tension in the air and rigidity in his big frame. Lola tried to slow her breathing, pushing her shoulders down.

'It follows on from our conversation on the beach,' he began and she nodded.

'I wanted to talk to you about that.' Lola smoothed her fingers over his knuckle. She'd spent years hiding her feelings and she was tired of it. She shot him a look, catching his gaze and feeling her pulse race. She wasn't naïve enough to think he'd fallen in love too, but she needed to know there was a chance for more.

'What we've shared has been wonderful, Niall. I've always cared for you, but these last weeks—'

'Please, Lola.' His finger touched her mouth, stopping her words. 'There's something I have to tell you first.'

Did he guess what she'd been going to say?

Did he know she loved him?

He didn't look like a man about to sweep her close and tell her he felt the same for her.

He looked like a man about to deliver tragic news.

Lola found herself watching their clasped hands, twined tight together, as if they each took strength from the other, knowing this was going to be bad.

'Say it, then.' She looked up and wished she couldn't see how hard this was for him. His features were drawn, his expression grim. Instinct told her she wouldn't like this, yet at the same time she wanted to smooth the frown from his brow and ease the pain she sensed in him.

It was easy to love a man who was strong, sexy and bold. Yet the tenderness welling inside her was no less, as she braced herself for the worst.

'You deserve someone better than me, Lola. I've always known it, and I suspect your family did too.'

She opened her mouth to protest that her family had loved him but his expression stopped her.

'What happened on the beach brought home to me how selfish I've been.' He turned his head slowly from side to side as if releasing stiff neck muscles, then rolled his shoulders. 'I knew from the start that I was no good for you. But I stopped thinking about it because I wanted you.'

His voice dropped to that low, resonant note she felt deep inside. Time and again he'd seduced her with his voice as much as his body. Yet now she heard pain, not seduction.

She lifted her hand to his jaw and he flinched. 'Don't, Lola. I don't deserve your tenderness.'

Yet for a moment he leaned into her palm before pulling away and setting his jaw. She dropped her hand, her heart falling too.

'You deserve a loving partner. Someone who'll always be there for you. Who can look after you and protect you and give you children if you want them.' His eyes locked on hers and she felt it like a flash of lightning striking to her heart. 'You want children, don't you?'

She nodded. 'One day, if I can.' She wasn't in a hurry, but she'd always imagined herself with a family.

'I can't. Or,' he said quickly when she went to speak, 'I *won't*. It wouldn't be right. I'm not cut out to have a family. I couldn't trust myself with a family.'

Lola frowned. 'I don't understand.' Niall was the most caring, protective man she knew. 'You'd make a wonderful husband and father.'

His shudder told its own story.

'Don't!' His voice was thick with distress. 'I'll never be that. I couldn't trust myself, or ask others to put their trust in me.' His eyes met hers, inky dark and stark with pain. 'My sister and my mother both died because of me.'

CHAPTER THIRTEEN

Lola stared at him, trying to make sense of the words that fell between them, as searing and heavy as drops of molten lead.

'You had a sister?'

Had Ed known? Her parents? She'd never suspected. But then Niall had never spoken about his family. Even when she was little, Lola had learned never to ask about his home life because he withdrew into himself.

Why had she never wondered about that? Never questioned Ed? It was just something she'd taken for granted.

Niall inclined his head, his throat working as if he had as much trouble swallowing as she did.

'Catriona. Younger than me. She had bright red hair and a cheeky smile.'

Lola was instantly reminded of the little girl on the beach. Was that why Niall had frozen? For a second she'd imagined she saw panic in his eyes, though later she'd told herself she imagined it.

'You spent a lot of time with her.' It was there in

his voice, in the curve of his mouth when he mentioned his sister. So much for his supposed inexperience with children.

'My parents were busy. I looked after her most of the time when I wasn't at school.'

'In Melbourne?'

He shook his head. 'I moved there with my father. After.'

Niall's jaw set like stone, as did the big thigh muscle beneath their joined hands. Yet she felt the tiny tremors running through him.

'How old was she, Niall?'

'Four. I was nine.' He breathed deep. 'It was late afternoon. We were playing in the hall when Dad told us to go outside because we were too noisy.' He paused. 'I think our parents were arguing again and didn't want us to hear. So we went out and Catriona asked me to show her how to ride the scooter I'd got for Christmas.'

Lola's heart dipped at his expression.

'We had a long driveway running down the side of the house so I taught her there, where I'd learned. She got the hang of it quickly and kept wanting to go further and faster. But she was a good kid and listened when I said she couldn't go out of our garden onto the footpath.'

Niall stopped then finally continued. She could see how much it cost him. 'I got distracted, just for a minute, I swear. I thought Mum called me and I turned around to check. When I turned back it was too late. All I can think is that Catriona intended to stop when she reached the footpath but there was a bump there and instead of stopping she careered out of control straight onto the street. Just as a car came past.'

'Oh, Niall!' Lola leaned against him, her arm going around his back, tears of horror and sympathy glazing her vision.

'Some nights I still hear the sound of those brakes. And Mum screaming.'

Lola tugged her hand free of his and looped both her arms around him. It didn't matter that he was bigger and stronger than her. She held him close, whispering words of comfort. Nonsense words, probably, but it didn't matter. All that mattered was the raw hurt he still felt and the need to ease it.

Eventually Niall lifted her up and settled her across his lap. They clutched each other tight, rocking together.

'It wasn't your fault, Niall. You were just a child. It was an accident.'

She felt him shake his head. 'It's no excuse. It was my job to look after her. That's what I always did. But because I wasn't paying attention, Catriona died.'

Lola opened her mouth then snapped it shut. Would it really help to tell him that if there was fault anywhere it was with his parents, who'd set a nine-year-old to watch his little sibling so they had privacy for an argument? It was the sort of awful accident no one could foresee.

Did this explain his protective attitude to her? From the first Niall had looked out for her. Yet she suspected it was a trait he'd carried before Catriona's death.

She felt him take a deep breath. 'After that my parents barely spoke and when they did it was to argue. Finally they separated. Mum got the short straw and took me with her. Dad moved to Melbourne.'

The short straw? Surely a bereaved mother would cleave even closer to her remaining child?

'Things weren't good. She blamed me for Catriona, naturally.' He broke off but Lola heard his ragged breathing, felt it in the rough movements of his chest.

'It *wasn't* your fault, Niall. Surely someone, a counsellor or other family members, made that clear?'

It was horrible to think of his mother blaming him. Was that why he still felt guilty? Anger swelled that a little kid should be made to carry that burden.

'Looking back now, I realise she was severely depressed. I was a reminder of what she'd lost and she couldn't move on. I could never be enough for her. I wasn't a solace but a torture to her.' He paused and Lola felt a horrible anticipation of worse to come. 'When I was eleven I came home from school to find her on the floor, dead from an overdose of prescription drugs.'

'Oh, Niall. That's appalling. I'm so sorry.'

To have a parent inflict such an experience on their child!

He held her tight and Lola nestled into his embrace, hugging him, trying to provide physical comfort when words were insufficient.

The way he spoke, the carefully neutral tone, was at odds with his rigidity and his tight embrace.

This, she realised, was the Niall she knew. Who hid his deepest feelings from the world. Just as, in his youth, he'd hidden them behind a spiky, combative attitude, and later, in his absorption with computers and passion for martial arts.

'If Catriona hadn't died, if I'd kept her safe the way I was supposed to, my mother wouldn't have killed herself.'

Lola pulled back in his arms, unable to sit still any longer. Hands cupping his face, she looked into his wounded dark eyes.

'You're *not* responsible for her death, Niall. You're not responsible for either one.'

His mouth lifted in a crumpled curve that hollowed her insides. 'You look so fierce, Lola. But it doesn't matter. It's too late now. I'll always carry that guilt.'

'Don't say that!'

It couldn't be too late for him. She refused to think it.

Lola leaned in and kissed him hard. So hard her teeth mashed his until he opened his mouth enough to let her in. She leaned in, kissing him with all the love in her heart, as if somehow she could undo years of misguided guilt.

Finally, breathless, she pulled back, planting her hands on his shoulders.

Lola felt furious with herself, forcing a kiss on him. As if that could magically change things! Furious with his mother, who'd taken her grief out on her little boy. Furious with his father, who hadn't been there to support them.

But what was the point of so much anger? How could she understand the grief that had torn the family apart?

Lola knew grief. It had taken over her life when her mother died. But to lose a child, or in Niall's case, to lose his family...

She looked into his eyes and read sorrow and regret. And knew, with a leaden heart, it wasn't only for the past, but for *them*. Because he believed his past made it impossible to share a future. He felt himself unworthy of love, of family.

Words formed in her head but none were the right ones. None would convince this wounded, caring, stubborn man that he deserved a future with someone who loved him. How could any platitude of hers convince him?

'What happened to your father?' It wasn't what

she really wanted to know. But it was better than the silence.

'I moved in with him till I left school. By then he had a new family, a wife and the first of their babies on the way.' He shrugged. 'We don't see each other now.'

There was finality in his words, as if warning her not to go there. Had they drifted apart or had his father pushed him away when he started a new family, rejecting his grieving son?

Fury roiled inside her at the way Niall had been turned into a scapegoat, made to pay for a tragic accident by adults who should have known better. She pushed it down. Giving vent to fruitless anger wouldn't help the man she loved.

'So, you see, Lola, I'm not cut out for a family. I'm not good at it and I'd never trust myself, or ask someone to trust me in that way. Do you understand?'

She nodded, her throat constricting as if caught in a noose.

'You're special.' His smile cut through her, because it held no happiness. 'You deserve to have the best life can give you, with the right man.' He breathed slowly. 'I needed to tell you, so you understood. I feel closer to you than I've felt with—' He shook his head as if regretting the words, leaving Lola to wonder what he'd meant to say. Closer than to any other woman? Her yearning heart beat faster.

'I always make it clear from the start that I can

only do short-term relationships. Except with you.'
He pushed her hair back from her face and her insides twisted at the tenderness of the gesture. 'I
should never have touched you. What we've shared
has been wonderful, but it can't go anywhere. You
need to know that. I've never shared this with anyone else.'

Lola blinked up at him.

All this time and he'd never shared this?

Pain filled her as she thought of him bearing all
this alone. The backs of her eyes turned gritty and
hot but she refused to cry. He'd probably blame himself then for hurting her!

Niall carried an impossible burden. He was
scared of hurting those he cared for. The only saving
grace was that he *did* care. He'd cared for his family, far more than his parents deserved, she couldn't
help feeling.

He cared for her, if not in the way she wanted.
She'd seen him interact with friends and acquaintances at the party and occasionally elsewhere in
the last couple of weeks, and he'd revealed himself
to be generous and warm-hearted.

It was a tragic waste that a man like Niall couldn't
move on and trust himself as he deserved.

'Thank you for telling me, Niall.'

Was it imagination or did he relax a little at
her words?

'Though I disagree with you.' She lifted her hand
when he would have interrupted. 'I hear what you're

saying. I understand why you think the way you do. But I don't believe for a second that you're unworthy of love or can't be trusted with a family of your own.'

'Lola.' His voice held a warning and his hands moved to her hips as if to dislodge her from his lap.

'Hear me out, Niall, just once.'

For a long moment he didn't respond, then finally nodded his head abruptly.

'We all blame ourselves when things go wrong. When my mother died I fretted about all the things I might have done differently that would have saved her.'

'You can't—'

She pressed her fingers to his lips. 'I know. It's madness to think that way, but for a while I circled back to it again and again.' Just as she'd wondered if she could have prevented her father's gambling. 'With time, and support, you'd have realised that. But you didn't get that support.' She swallowed the bitter words on her tongue. 'Instead you suffered a second tragedy, not of your making.'

Niall's mouth tightened but he said nothing.

'I know you, Niall. My whole family knew you and trusted you. Do you really think my parents would have given the run of the house to a boy who might endanger me? If anything, you've always been more protective than Ed.'

'Because I know how easily things can go wrong.'

Lola nodded. 'Exactly, don't you see? Things *go*

wrong. It's not always a matter of blame. You did the best you could. You thought your mother called so of course you turned around. You're not to blame for what happened. To think that you don't deserve happiness is just plain wrong.'

For a second Lola wondered if she'd got through to him. But this mindset was ingrained. He was just being patient and polite while he heard her out.

'Thank you, Lola. I know you mean well.' He paused. 'I'll always be available if you need help. Either you or Ed. So long as you understand that this, between us, was a mistake. We should never have become intimate.'

Her chin jerked up. 'Because you can't trust me not to become needy and dependent?'

She shot to her feet, torn between hurt that he was so obstinate and anger at herself for falling for a man so determined to dwell in the past. She *did* feel needy and dependent.

'I did my share of seducing,' she snapped. 'Promise me that you won't add *Seducing Lola* to the list of things you feel guilty about. You're already burdened with enough.'

She sounded grumpy but couldn't help it. They'd found something special but Niall was hell-bent on self-sacrifice.

'Lola, listen, I—'

'If you don't mind, let's postpone the rest of the lecture on why you're no good for me till later. I've got a bit of a headache and want to lie down.'

She turned away, fearing he'd reach out and stop her, which would be disastrous because he'd see the tears she fought, clinging to her lashes.

But he didn't say a word. Nor did he follow.

Niall expected that from then on Lola would keep her distance.

He'd underestimated her.

An hour later she joined him in the kitchen, where he'd been staring into the fridge, telling himself he should organise a meal for them, but unable to focus.

His thoughts were a jumble. Taken up with the past, but, more importantly, with the sight, sound, scent and feel of Lola, sitting on his lap, holding him tight and telling him it wasn't his fault. That he wasn't the damned soul he'd always believed. That he had a right to expect more.

His chest ached and there was a hard, tight nugget of something lodged behind his ribs that wouldn't shift.

Then she walked into the kitchen, as if nothing had happened, and took over organising their meal.

Almost as if nothing had happened, because her gaze never quite met his and her smile was a dim facsimile of her usual one.

That was when Niall discovered he was a coward. For he didn't force conversation back to their earlier discussion. Instead he fetched the spices she demanded for her marinade, searched out a white wine to accompany the chicken, and fired the charcoal barbecue.

A stranger would have thought the scene companionable as they worked together, her preparing a spicy salad while he cooked the marinated meat, then sat, eating and looking out into the dusky evening.

But Niall felt the difference. There was a new constraint between them and Lola's eyes looked different. As if the light had gone out behind them.

He'd done the right thing, warning her of his true nature and setting boundaries that should have been spelled out long before. Yet that didn't make it any easier.

He was weak where she was concerned. The fact he'd given in to his physical craving for her, despite the dictates of his conscience, was proof. How could he entertain thoughts of a future with Lola, or trust himself to care for her as she deserved, when he couldn't even summon the strength to resist her?

He'd been so tempted to believe her persuasive words. Because he wanted, badly, for them to be true. No one had ever shown such absolute trust in him personally, not just in his business acumen. She had such faith, even admiration. He'd wondered if maybe redemption were possible. Could Lola's belief in him make a difference?

The thought was short-lived. It would kill him if he again lost someone he cared for through his own neglect. He couldn't take that risk, not with Lola.

They washed up together, utterly rational, polite companions, but Niall couldn't take any more.
Being close to Lola, but not close enough, knowing
he'd never be close enough again, was too much.

He excused himself, saying he had to finish some
work prior to a meeting he had to attend in Brisbane
tomorrow. Yet when he got to his office he couldn't
settle. Didn't even open his computer. Just stood,
staring into the night.

That was where Lola found him. She didn't say
anything, just walked over and curved her hand
through his arm, pulling him towards the door.

'Lola, I can't—'

'Shh.' Her fingers skimmed his mouth and that
tantalising touch made his throat convulse. 'Don't
overthink this, Niall. We both need company.
That's all.'

Minutes later they were in bed, bodies tangling
and breathing heavy, their eyes locked as they used
hands and mouths to give each other pleasure and
eventually release.

Then Niall played the coward again, closing his
eyes and pretending to sleep because he feared what
he might let slip if he spoke to Lola in this un-
guarded state. That he might forget what she needed
and deserved and think only of his selfish desire to
keep her close.

Lola woke in the early hours. Even in sleep it was
as if Niall protected her, cradling her against his

chest. She shifted her weight and he must have been awake, for he lifted his hand in a slow caress.

He brought her to arousal so fast her head would have spun if she weren't lying across him.

Lola blinked back searing heat and tried not to think about anything but the moment. The simple joy of carnal desire. They made love again silently, with the ease of long-time lovers, yet with an urgency that made it feel like the first time.

Or the last.

Niall's touch was infinitely tender yet devastatingly arousing. Within minutes they were locked together, bodies melding, hearts beating in unison, as if they'd been made for such moments.

The thought didn't bring its usual magic, instead awakening her impatience at this stubborn, stoic man who'd made self-abnegation an art form. She clawed at his shoulders, biting down on his neck, feeling his powerful body jerk in response.

Their lovemaking changed. Became less perfect, less easy, turning into a wild, no-holds-barred plunge of two beings driven by desperation.

Her orgasm came hard and fast, almost before she realised. Niall's came at the same time. She saw him arch, head flung back as he pumped into her. His mouth moved, silently forming her name.

That was when Lola broke, closing her eyes against the tears she couldn't let fall, holding tight to the man she loved, knowing he would never let her be his.

CHAPTER FOURTEEN

'Ms Suarez?'

Lola yawned and pushed her tangled hair off her face. She'd had too little sleep, fretting over Niall and his determination to end their relationship. He'd left at dawn this morning, driving to Brisbane for a day of meetings, his demeanour telling her nothing had changed.

'Yes? Speaking.'

'Inspector Corcoran here.'

Lola stiffened, leaning against the kitchen counter where she waited for her tea to brew. She'd *thought* she recognised the voice.

'Inspector.' She swallowed. 'You have some news?'

'Yes, I do.' He paused and she wondered what was coming. 'There's been an incident. Jayden Braithwaite is dead.'

'Dead?' She blinked, trying to get her mind into gear. 'Braithwaite is dead? You're sure it's him?'

'Yes, his identity's been confirmed.'

The rest of his words blurred as her legs gave way and she slid down to the floor.

'Ms Suarez? Are you still there?'

The voice sounded far away and she realised belatedly that the phone was on the floor, grasped in her white-knuckled grip. She shook all over and it took conscious effort to lift the phone to her ear.

'I'm sorry, Inspector. I missed that. Would you mind repeating what you said?'

Twenty minutes later, phone still gripped in her hand, Lola got to her feet. She tipped out the cold, stewed tea and boiled the kettle again.

She felt calm now, almost unnaturally so. After that first wave of reaction, her emotions had flattened out completely. It felt as if everything were happening a long way away, or to someone else.

It seemed Niall's insistence on posting someone in Lola's flat had finally borne fruit, luring Braithwaite into action. Last night another attempt had been made to get into her home, but the security Niall had organised, and the alert presence of her body double, had foiled that.

The police had arrived just too late to catch Braithwaite and he hadn't returned to his boarding house. Instead, hours later, the police had been called to an explosion in a supposedly derelict warehouse. The theory was that, angry at his close shave trying to enter her apartment, Braithwaite had grown impatient and careless. Experts said he'd been planning a letter bomb that had accidentally detonated. In addition to the remains of the explosive device, they found an envelope addressed to her, plus the equipment he'd used earlier to monitor her flat.

No, the inspector said, there was no doubt it was Braithwaite. There was no doubt he'd been planning more harm. And there was no reason now for her to remain in Queensland.

No reason except Niall was here and she feared that if she left she'd never see him again.

The kettle clicked off and she busied herself, making tea. Ignoring the splintering cracks in her unnatural calm as shock started to wear off. A shaft of pain pierced her and she sucked in her breath, trying to stifle it.

She loved Niall. What she felt wasn't infatuation or a crush. Once upon a time, perhaps, but not now.

But he didn't feel that way about her. Worse, he'd believed in his guilt and unworthiness for so long, she feared she'd never convince him to take a chance on them as a couple.

Her mouth twisted as she added milk to her tea and took a sip.

A screech sounded outside and she looked up to see lorikeets squabbling in the trees, their colours blurring. It took a moment to realise the hazy focus came from the moisture welling in her eyes.

So much for feeling numb!

Lola cradled her tea and looked out at the view she'd come to love.

What could she do? Stay here and try to persuade Niall that he was wrong, and that what they shared was worth keeping alive? She wouldn't talk in terms of permanency because he'd shut her down instantly. But if she could persuade him to keep going as they were…

Then what?

Give up your job and your life in Melbourne in hopes Niall might one day see sense?

Live on a knife edge, waiting for the day he decides it's not working and you need to separate?

Lola gulped down tea, feeling it scald her throat.

She was tired of feeling vulnerable around Niall. It had to stop.

She'd spent years pining for the impossible. Hoping Niall would one day notice her, or that some stranger would live up to the impossible ideal she'd built in her head.

Niall wasn't the hero she'd imagined. He was close to it, so very close, but he was flawed like everyone else. His vision of himself was so skewed he didn't dare believe he could be happy with anyone. Which meant he couldn't offer her even a hope of a future together.

Lola didn't expect promises of for ever straight away, but she wanted the chance for that. She wanted to love a man who might one day love her back.

Niall cared for her. He wanted to protect her.

But he didn't love her. Chances were he never would.

Which meant she only had one choice.

Turning her back on the riot of colour and sound in the treetops, she carried her tea to the bedroom and her packing.

During his early drive to Brisbane Niall received a report that Braithwaite had tried to enter Lola's flat the previous night but got away.

Blood chilling, he'd demanded details. Disappointment at the man's escape vied with relief that Lola's body double was okay. And that Lola was safe here in Queensland.

The thought of losing another person he cared about, someone he was responsible for…the idea was unthinkable.

About to do a U-turn and head back to Lola and the mountain house, he stopped. Logic decreed she was safe since Braithwaite believed her to be in Melbourne. Yet the urge to be with her was strong.

Except she'd be hurt and annoyed at what she'd see as Niall's overprotectiveness.

So he forced himself to keep going, arriving early for the negotiations that had been months in the planning. Yet he couldn't dispel the disquiet gnawing at his gut.

Mid-morning, during a break in the negotiations, came the information that Braithwaite was dead. At first Niall couldn't believe it. The news of the planned letter bomb curdled his gut. If Lola had been there, defenceless…

But she hadn't been. She was alive and well.

Relief slammed into him, an overwhelming wave, rocking him back on his heels.

Lola wouldn't have to look over her shoulder worrying about a malevolent stalker.

He called her but went straight to her message bank.

She was probably busy, talking to the cops.

There was nothing to worry about. She was safe.

Yet, behind the crashing wave of relief loomed something else. Something exacerbated by the fact he wasn't able to talk with her. An overwhelming sense of—could it be?—anxiety.

'Mr Pedersen? We're resuming in the conference room now.'

Niall nodded but stayed where he was, staring at the phone in his hand, trying to identify the reason for his unease.

He should be celebrating. He'd kept Lola safe from Braithwaite. Yet he didn't feel triumphant or even mildly satisfied. Instead a cold weight filled his belly.

Lola has no reason to stay now.

Why would she stay with a man like you? She knows the truth about you now.

You could never be right for a woman like her.

A woman who deserved and, he guessed, wanted, more than a short affair. He could imagine Lola with children. With a stellar career and a doting husband.

Pain spiked in his jaw at the thought of her smiling at some nameless, faceless man. Being with him in the ways she'd been with Niall. Sharing her future.

He swallowed and somehow the pain in his jaw transferred to his throat. It felt as if it were studded with nails.

Niall couldn't allow himself to think about a future with anyone. He knew his limitations. Knew that eventually he'd let her down. Catastrophe followed him as night followed day, which was why he kept his personal relationships short. The idea of losing Lola through some mistake he'd made, some error of judgement or fleeting distraction…

So why did the thought of her leaving fill him with dread?

Not just dread, but a terrible ache as if from a physical blow.

Fear of abandonment?

Not likely! He'd come to terms years before with the loss of his family, two dead and one uncaring of the severed bond between them. His father had been eager to forget the son responsible for destroying their family unit, concentrating on his new wife and children.

Niall was used to being alone.

He didn't need anyone. Just as no one needed him.

Keep telling yourself that, Pedersen.

'Niall?' It was his chief legal advisor. 'We need you.'

'Coming.'

He thumbed in a text to Lola and returned to the conference room.

Never had a meeting dragged so much. Especially a negotiation that promised a significant and lucrative expansion of business.

Yet Niall couldn't concentrate. More than once he caught his team frowning at him, wondering at his abstraction. Fortunately they were well prepared and the discussions proceeded as planned.

In the next break, Niall dragged out his phone before anyone could accost him. Still Lola didn't answer. Nor had she returned his text.

Fear skated down his spine.

He rang his housekeeper, only to discover she was out of the area for the day. He was on the point of ringing Pedersen Security staff on the Gold Coast, to ask them to...

What? Drive up the mountain and check she was okay?

Braithwaite was dead. Lola wasn't in danger.

Yet instinct told him they needed to speak.

Not just to hear how she was doing with this news about her stalker, but because of what he'd told her yesterday.

He'd revealed his history, waiting for the moment she'd shy away from him, horrified. But she hadn't. She'd held him and kissed him. Kissed him! As if *he* were the victim, not the one responsible.

Niall had come to think of Lola as practical and clear-sighted, but he'd reckoned without her soft heart. Her response had thrown him, almost made him forget his vow to keep her safe. Safe even from him.

Instead of keeping her distance, she'd led him to bed! And he, weak where Lola was concerned, had taken everything she offered, losing himself in her sweet body and generous loving. Not once but several times.

Was it any wonder he'd left while she was barely awake, using his Brisbane meeting as an excuse?

Because in the grey, dawn light he knew he'd have to find the strength to walk away from her. For her own good.

Another call straight to message bank. Another text she didn't answer.

Pinching the bridge of his nose, trying to ease his rising panic, Niall searched out the head of his legal team, instructing him on the rest of the deal. Then, before the lawyer could do more than gape, Niall took the stairs to the basement car park at a gallop rather than wait for the lift. Minutes later he was in his car, heading to the mountains.

He was too late.

The house was empty. Lola was gone.

Yet it was Niall who felt empty, standing before her empty wardrobe. Completely hollow, as if a slight breeze might knock him off his feet.

He'd known grief and loss. Yet he hadn't been prepared for this. Niall told himself it was for the best but it was no consolation.

He found her note on the kitchen bench. The island bench where, more than once, they'd made love because they couldn't bear to wait to get to a bedroom.

Holding his breath, he opened the folded page.

Niall scanned it rapidly, searching for a reference to seeing him again. But his eyes snagged on phrases that made the hair stand up on the back of his neck and his breath stop.

...care for you deeply...
...move on with my life. It's been on hold far too long, because of my feelings for you.

He'd had no idea. Could it be true?

Lola, caring for him all this time? Lola hoping...

His heart hammered as he thought back over everything she'd said and done, how she'd looked and acted, but already he was reading on. What he read made his heart stutter then plunge in a descent that didn't seem to stop.

...understand you're scared of losing someone you care for.

He'd always known Lola was insightful. Even as a kid she'd seen more than many of the people around her. But the simplicity with which she named his fear stunned him.

Niall braced himself on the granite countertop,

vaguely aware of his laboured breaths and the hard pump of his lungs.

He *was* scared of getting close to someone and letting them down. Because of him Catriona had died. Because of that his parents split up and his mother killed herself. In her final years, whenever she looked at him he'd seen blame and despair in her eyes.

Yet Lola made his fear sound like cowardice, not prudence or the need to protect others from his flawed self.

He swallowed hard, pain scraping his gullet.

Could she be right?

He couldn't think like that. It was the sort of wishful thinking that could undo him. Or endanger someone special, like Lola.

You deserve more from life and I do too. So I'm moving on.

Goodbye, Niall.

There was no signature. No trite words about seeing him later.

Goodbye.

She meant for ever.

Lola was doing what he'd hoped, severing ties. Leaving him so he couldn't harm her any more.

His head spun with the idea that she'd had feelings for him all this time. That because of him, she'd held herself back from being with other men.

Stupidly, he felt a leap of excitement that it hadn't just been primal sexual attraction for her. That she cared profoundly.

Until he recalled what that meant. Caring equated in his experience with vulnerability. Love with death and grief. He couldn't be selfish enough to want her...*attached* to him in that way.

Could he?

Of course not.

Yet as he held the paper her words blurred and he felt an ache behind his eyes and at the back of his throat that he hadn't felt since he was eleven. When he'd watched them lower a coffin into the ground and grieved the mother who'd no longer loved him.

This was for the best. Lola would be safe now, without him.

CHAPTER FIFTEEN

THREE WEEKS LATER, on a sunny spring Saturday, Lola moved into her new flat. It was further out from the city centre but the neighbourhood had a good vibe and there were no bad memories to send a shiver down her spine when she came home late from work.

Bending at the knees, she lifted a box of books for the big bookcase. Once she put her pictures and books up it would feel more like home. She ignored the inner voice that told her she was kidding herself.

How could any place feel like home when she'd left her heart behind in Queensland?

It sounded corny, but it was true.

She just had to close her eyes to see Niall's face when he'd revealed his past. His pain as he told her he was to blame for what happened to his family, impressing upon her that she deserved better than a man like him.

There was a gaping hole where her heart had torn open.

She'd wanted to help him. Encourage him to

understand he wasn't to blame and that the future could be bright for them both if he'd only take the risk and trust himself. As he'd insisted she trust him when she was in danger.

But life wasn't that easy, was it? Even for a man who was scarily clear-sighted in other things, like building an internationally renowned business in a decade, he had a blind spot about his past.

If it had been easy, Niall would have believed her. Lola imagined him reading the note explaining her feelings and realising he felt the same. He'd have jumped on his private jet and beaten her back to Melbourne.

Foolishly, when she'd arrived she'd scanned the arrivals hall for his tall figure. She'd half expected to hear him calling her name, because he couldn't let her go.

The last weeks she'd gone through the motions. Her friends and colleagues hadn't seemed to notice. Maybe they thought she was shaken up by what had happened with Braithwaite.

She worked hard, even managed to contribute sensibly to her new team project. She'd organised a new place to live in record time because she no longer felt comfortable in her old one.

Lola had told herself that was why sleep proved elusive. But it was a lie. She'd lain awake thinking of Niall. Wanting him and wishing he could move on from his past. But she didn't have the professional skills to help him understand he was a victim in his family's tragedy, not its cause.

She'd always seen his drive and determination as strengths but now she cursed his obstinacy. He was so wedded to guilt he couldn't move past it.

Putting the box down, Lola sighed and stretched, forcing her thoughts from Niall. New place, new start. No more foolish dreams. No more—

The intercom from the building's main entrance sounded and she frowned. She'd turned down a couple of offers from friends to help unpack because after a week at work she was tired of putting on a front. Smiling made her face sore and it was tough pretending everything was okay when she wondered if she'd ever be okay again.

'Yes?'

Silence for a second that made her wonder if someone had keyed in the wrong flat number.

'Hello, Lola.'

Shock pressed her back against the wall, her hand to her throat as if to hold down the pulse leaping there.

'Niall?' Her voice sounded scratchy.

'Can I come up?'

No, no, no!

That's the last thing you need. How are you going to forget him if you...?

Lola pushed the button that opened the main entrance. So much for listening to caution!

'I'm at number—'

'Twenty, I know.'

He knew? How?

Did it matter? With his resources it would be child's play to discover her address. The easiest way would have been to ask her. But he hadn't. He hadn't been in contact. She'd assumed he didn't intend to see her again.

Yet now here he was.

Lola smoothed down her shirt, a little grimy from hauling boxes, then realised she was primping.

She set her jaw. No more. She couldn't cut off her feelings for Niall as if they'd never been, but she wouldn't go back to hoping for more than he could give. She'd spent too long doing that and look where it had got her. With an aching heart and a dead feeling inside, as if part of her had been amputated.

Drawing a deep breath, she went to the door, opening it just as Niall appeared, striding up the stairs two at a time, the picture of lean energy.

Her pulse thrummed and a boulder lodged in her throat. She swallowed. 'Is there a problem with the lift?'

He lifted his head as he took the last couple of steps, his gaze cutting straight to hers. Lola was glad to lean against the doorjamb because her stupid legs turned wobbly.

'It was slow.'

Part of her wanted to see that as proof he was eager to see her. The new, saner Lola said Niall had always had energy to burn. It was nothing personal.

'Can I come in?' He was before her now, looking obscenely delectable in faded jeans that outlined his powerful thighs and a dark shirt the colour of his eyes, the sleeves rolled up.

It was one thing to tell herself she was strong. An entirely other thing to feel it when that dark blue gaze snared hers.

'Why?' She stood straight, folding her arms across her chest. But her determination wilted as she took in the sharp set of his features. He looked as if he'd lost weight, those beautiful, pared features edging towards gaunt.

Lola blinked. No time now for imaginings.

Yet as she stared, she noticed tiny vertical lines above his nose that she'd swear hadn't been there before, and the grooves bracketing his mouth surely scored deeper.

'It won't take long, but it's important.'

His expression revealed nothing, a reminder that when it came to negotiating and getting his way, Niall was in a league of his own.

He probably wants to check you're fine so he can report to Ed then finally wash his hands of you.

Because they had nothing else to say to each other. Lola's mouth twisted and pain corkscrewed down through her middle.

Finally, because she probably owed him her life, Lola nodded. 'Come in.'

He moved swiftly. He was in her flat, moving down the hallway before she could blink.

In a hurry to get this over. Well, that suited her.

The lounge room was full of boxes and there was nowhere to sit but she wasn't going to invite him into her bedroom, the only room she'd finished, right down to fresh sheets on the bed.

'Nice place.'

Her eyebrows rose. The place looked a wreck at the moment and the whole flat would fit inside just one of the elegant sitting rooms in his mountain retreat.

Lola narrowed her eyes and saw the jerky movement as he swallowed. Could it possibly be that Niall was nervous? Now she really was imagining things.

He watched Lola cross her arms, reinforcing the barriers between them.

Even so he had the devil's own job not eating her up with his eyes. The press of her breasts against the thin white shirt alone threatened to undo him. He saw the outline of her white bra. Was that a familiar tiny red bow between her breasts?

Instantly he wondered if she wore the cute panties dotted with cherries beneath her close-fitting jeans.

Heat smothered his skin as erotic images bombarded him, but he squashed them with the devastating knowledge she didn't want him here. It was branded in her stance, the hitched-high shoulders, the tilted chin and downturned mouth. She didn't even bother to break the ice by offering refreshments, which in her family was tantamount to a deliberate insult.

Niall swallowed again, pain scouring from his throat down to his abdomen.

Had he really expected a welcome?

'What do you want, Niall?'

'I had to see you and—'

'Of course,' she interrupted. 'To check I'm okay. It's what you do, isn't it? Because you promised Ed. And, presumably, to check I was satisfied with your firm's service before you sign the task off as completed.'

She laughed and his nerves jangled at the note of bitterness. He'd never heard Lola sound like that.

'You can put your mind at rest. They, you, did a sterling job. If ever anyone I know needs protection, I'll be sure to recommend Pedersen Security. I might even write an online review.'

She reduced what they'd shared to a *job*?

Out of the all-consuming blur of pain and doubt, made more terrible by the tiny bud of hope that had begun to form, indignation flared.

The likelihood of him getting what he wanted was minuscule. Niall knew coming here was a triumph of desperation over sense. But he refused to let Lola relegate what he'd done to a mere job.

'I'd try to help anyone who found themselves in that situation.' He watched her stiffen. 'But don't ever pretend, even to yourself, that I protected you as a job or solely out of a sense of obligation to Ed.'

He sucked in a searing breath. 'Yes, I owe your family a debt I can never repay. Yes, Ed's my best mate and there's not much I wouldn't do for him. But I *care* for you.'

It wasn't the way he'd planned to say it. He'd practised a softly, softly approach, slowly winning her over, not arguing.

'Oh, you *care*, Niall, just not enough.' She uncrossed her arms, shifted her weight and recrossed them. For a second he saw vulnerability in her shadowed eyes and taut mouth, and that tiny bud of hope grew a little.

He closed the space between them in two strides, watching surprise freeze her features.

'I care more than I can say.' His voice hit a gravel rumble and he had to pause as feelings, all those feelings he'd once strived to suppress, bubbled up in a churning, confused mass.

Niall touched her arms, his hands closing gently on her elbows. Then, discovering how she trembled, he ran his palms up to her shoulders with some vague idea of soothing or supporting her. Which would have made sense if his hands weren't unsteady too.

'I can't...' He shook his head impatiently. 'I'm not good with the words, Lola. Not about emotions.' For most of his life strong emotion had equated to pain and regret. To self-disgust. And because whatever words of love his parents had ever bestowed were long forgotten under the weight of guilt.

She didn't say anything to help him, just watched mutely. But as he stared back Niall saw her hazel eyes glitter brighter. Her breasts rose high with each shallow breath as if she, too, found breathing difficult.

'I'm scared,' he confessed and saw her frown. 'Scared that I'll let you down, or that your feelings have changed. But even so I couldn't keep away. I need you, Lola, in ways I'd never imagined before.'

The strength of that need stunned him. He'd spent three weeks battling the urge to follow her, trying to find a way to shore up his determination to keep away.

But with Lola he'd tasted Paradise, not just in bed, but in her loving warmth. And he found that, after all, he was a weak man, too weak to stay away.

'Oh, Niall!' Her hands gripped his arms and another tiny tendril shot out from that bud of hope.

Except she didn't sound happy. She sounded torn.

'Lola.' Even her name was a benediction. 'I don't want to hurt you. If you don't want me any more I'll go and you'll never see me again.'

'Don't you…dare.'

It was a whisper, barely heard over his rushing pulse. Niall tilted his head closer, reading the glow in her eyes.

'You still want me?' Despite every hope it seemed impossible. Niall had been alone so long, all his life it seemed. So the idea of this one, marvellous woman believing in him, trusting him, seemed un-fathomable.

'For a very clever man you can be so blind, Niall Pedersen. I've wanted you since I had braces and puppy fat.'

Disappointment vied with elation, 'Lola, what-ever pedestal you once put me on, I'm not that man.' Surely he'd made that clear? 'I'm deeply flawed.' Much as he wanted her, he couldn't let her throw her future away on a mirage. 'I shouldn't have touched you but I'm weak where you're concerned. I delayed telling you the truth about my past because I was selfish. I couldn't bear for you to turn away from me, even though I knew you should. Because being with you made me…'

Her eyebrows rose. 'Happy?'

He shook his head, lifting his hand to stroke her cheek. 'Far more than that, lovely Lola.' He drew a trembling breath. 'Happy. Content. Fulfilled. *Hopeful*. For the first time I felt…' he shook his head '…right. As if all these years a part of me was missing and I'd found it again.'

'Oh, Niall.' Her mouth worked and she blinked.

'Hell! Lola, I'm sorry. Don't cry, please.'

'I'm not crying, I'm happy. And before you warn me off again, I know full well that you're not per-fect. Neither of us are.'

Niall scowled down at her. He couldn't recall any of his girlfriends crying with happiness. Maybe it was the nature of the emotion that made the difference.

His emotions were all over the place, hope and excitement vying with fear and wonder.

'The problem is,' he made himself go on, needing to say this, 'I can't guarantee to make you happy.' Or to protect her as she deserved, but Niall had learned enough to know she didn't want to hear about him protecting her. 'I'd like to try though.'

He ignored the prickling between his shoulder blades, the reminder of past mistakes. It was the hardest thing he'd done in his life, trying to forge a new path, telling himself maybe Lola was right and he could find love. Putting the past behind him.

She opened her mouth then closed it again. Finally she spoke, her eyes locked on his. 'You'd like to make me happy because I make you feel hopeful and *right*?'

Niall's hopes dipped. It didn't sound enough, did it? He yanked in more air, wondering why his lungs wouldn't fill.

'I'm not much of a catch, I know.' Not with his emotional hang-ups. At her raised eyebrows he shook his head. 'Well, except for the money.'

Suddenly she was smiling and it was the most wonderful thing he'd seen in weeks. 'That's a lovely compliment, Niall. That you know I'm not interested in your money.'

He tried to think of something else to entice her, but all the smooth words he'd practised on the flight south had deserted him. There was just the truth, raw and unvarnished.

Soft fingers brushed his cheek, feathering to his jaw then lower, to splay around the back of his neck. He revelled in her touch.

'As for not being good with words—' she shook her head '—I disagree. Do you *really* feel like you've found a part of you that was missing?' Her eyes shone and gradually Niall's anxiety disappeared.

He cupped her face in both hands. 'I do. With you I feel hopeful. I feel...*love.*' That was the only possible explanation. 'I've tried to explain away my feelings for weeks but they wouldn't be explained away. I love you, Lola Suarez. I want to be with you. Long term.'

After years of telling lovers he was only interested in time-limited affairs, he needed to spell that out, and it felt good, far better than he'd expected.

He read excitement in Lola's eyes and the upward curve of her lips. 'You really mean it!'

Niall could no longer resist. He pressed a kiss to the corner of her smiling mouth. Then to the other corner. Somehow his arms were around her and she was kissing him back with a tender passion that was unique to Lola.

It felt wondrous.

Niall teetered on the brink of fear. Loving this woman made him vulnerable in ways he'd planned never to be vulnerable again. But it was too late for fear. Too late for anything but holding tight and trusting in their love for each other.

He pulled back, just enough to look into her hazel eyes. They sparkled like green gems and his heart thudded with pride and humility.

This woman loved him. Really, truly loved him.

The tender buds of hope branched out into a green garden, where once there'd been only wasteland.

'If you trust me, I'll do my best to be the sort of man you deserve.' It wouldn't be easy, he had so much to learn, but he was determined. With Lola, Niall had the best possible incentive.

'You already are that man, my love.' Her words carved their way through his very soul. She gazed up at him and what he read in her expression un-shackled the last chains around his heart. 'And I promise to do my best to be the sort of woman you deserve.'

'Sweet Lola,' he groaned. 'You're everything I want and need and far more than I deserve.'

He bent to kiss her again when she whispered, 'Did I mention that the only room that's finished is the bedroom? There are fresh sheets and...'

Lola never got to finish. His mouth found hers. Right now talking seemed like such a waste of time.

Still kissing, Niall swung her up into his arms and carried her into the bedroom, where he dem-onstrated his feelings for her in more tangible ways.

EPILOGUE

THE DOORS OPENED with their usual discreet hiss. With Niall's hand warm at her back, Lola stepped inside.

Awestruck, she gazed around her. 'Carolyn's outdone herself this time.'

She'd thought that after two years she was used to their hostess's wild extravagance. But the profusion of colourful silks and glittering, overflowing treasure chests dazzled the eyes. The multi-storey atrium was dominated by an enormous ship's mast, complete with bright sails and a sequinned pirate flag. The rigging was made of golden chains studded with faux gems and the sails and flag billowed in the breeze created by concealed fans.

Niall chuckled. 'Do you think she could have fitted in any more bling?'

'I doubt it, darling.' Their hostess's amused voice came from nearby. 'Poor Ted's been wearing his sunglasses inside since we set up.' Her throaty laugh engulfed them as she hugged Lola. Then she kissed

Niall on the cheek and with a wink at Lola added, 'Any excuse to kiss your delicious man, darling.'

Lola smiled as Niall reached for her hand, threading their fingers together. That familiar jolt shot through her.

The thrill of being with the man she loved hadn't worn off. She doubted it ever would. Especially when he gave her that special smile he reserved just for her. The smile of a man who loved her and was no longer afraid to admit it.

She heard a sigh and turned back to Carolyn, taking in for the first time the full impact of her costume.

'You approve?' Carolyn batted her eyelashes as Lola grinned and Niall laughed.

'It's truly memorable,' Lola offered. 'Only you could carry it off with such style.'

Anyone else would look comical wearing a ruby studded eyepatch, skin-tight black silk trousers tucked into high-heeled boots and a white silk shirt that fell in enormous flounces and ruffles. But Carolyn had the necessary panache to carry off even the sequinned, toy parrot on her shoulder. The rubies at her throat and the jewel-studded sword by her hip only added to overall effect.

'Thank you, darling. But I'd trade it all for that glow of yours. You look gorgeous.' She looked from one to the other. 'As for you, Niall, settling down suits you. It's a delight to see you both so happy.'

A man in a satin frock coat and breeches called

and Carolyn turned. 'Sorry, my dears. I'm needed. Catering, you know. I'll see you later.'

They stood for a moment taking in the throng of pirates and women in corseted, long-skirted dresses mixing with others, like themselves, in more conventional dress.

'Not sorry you came?' Lola murmured. Society parties weren't really Niall's thing.

'Never.' He drew her through the vast space till they found a relatively quiet oasis from which to watch the revelry. 'Not when I'm with the most beautiful woman here.'

If anyone else had said that, Lola would have known it for flattery. But as Niall's hungry gaze traced her figure in her metallic green dress, she knew that he meant it. To him she was beautiful, just as to her he was the sexiest man on the planet. As well as the most loving.

A shiver of happiness passed through her.

'Cold?' He wrapped his arm around her and she leaned in.

'Not at all. Just thinking how lucky I am.'

His heated gaze morphed into something else. Something serious yet incredibly tender.

'That would be me, darling Lola. Lucky to have you.'

He lifted her left hand, a look of satisfaction on his face as he took in her gold wedding band and the deep lustre of the square-cut emerald on her engagement ring. He lifted her hand to his lips and joy fizzed in her blood.

It had been a year since their wedding on a secluded tropical beach, attended by her father and Ed and a handful of her friends and Niall's. In that year she and Niall had grown ever closer, dealing with the inevitable challenges two strong-willed people would face, joining their lives.

Yet they'd been willing to adapt and learn. Lola had sought counselling after the trauma of being stalked and Niall had finally done the same, finding a level of peace with his difficult past.

Nor had he tried to take over her life or make her decisions. She'd been dumbfounded when Niall moved to Melbourne to be with her, rearranging his business to achieve that. He could oversee his company from almost anywhere, he'd said, whereas she needed to be with her team while she pursued her new direction.

With her career taking off, she'd recently scored a promising junior advertising job in Queensland and they'd moved north. They spent weekdays in the city and weekends in Niall's mountain retreat or on the island hideaway he'd bought as a wedding gift.

'Life just gets better and better,' he murmured as he kissed her wrist, sending squiggles of delight through her.

'Really?' He seemed happy, but now and then she wondered if, despite his excitement, this week's news might be a step too far for the man who'd once thought himself destined to stay alone.

'Really.' Niall's other hand skimmed her abdomen, his smile so tender Lola forgot to breathe. 'It's true I'm nervous about becoming a father. I'll have to work hard at doing it well, but with you I feel up to the challenge. Together we make a great team.'

Lola placed her hand over his where it rested protectively over the new life inside her. 'My thoughts exactly.'

There it was again, the spark of emotion in his cobalt eyes that felt like a caress.

'Excellent.' He gathered her close in his arms. 'Now dance with me before I'm tempted to spirit you away.'

They had a wonderful evening, catching up with friends and making new acquaintances, enjoying convivial company and lavish entertainment.

But to Lola the best part of the night was the love in Niall's eyes and the joy of going home with him.

He was her friend, her lover, the father of her unborn baby. He was the light of her life and whatever the future held she knew they'd fight to make it good for each other and those they loved.

* * * * *

Loved the drama of
The Innocent's Protector in Paradise?
Fall in love with these other Annie West stories!

Claiming His Out-of-Bounds Bride
The King's Bride by Arrangement
The Sheikh's Marriage Proclamation
Pregnant with His Majesty's Heir
A Consequence Made in Greece

Available now!